"I need you to marry me."

Emily was looking at Kadir as if he'd grown two extra heads. He didn't blame her, really. What he was proposing was perfectly outrageous. But after that phone call with Rashid he couldn't stop thinking about how he wasn't going to be forced to take his brother's birthright.

And for that Kadir needed a very unsuitable bride. A woman who would hopefully persuade his father into believing his judgment was so poor he would not, under any circumstances, give the kingdom of Kyr into his keeping.

"I… I…" Emily raised a hand to push a stray lock of hair from her face and he was once more confronted with a fact he had somehow managed to ignore for the past four years.

Emily Bryant was not quite the unattractive automaton he'd believed her to be. Her brown hair was long, thick, and shiny—and very tumbled. He'd never seen it down before.

And now her mouth had somehow become enticing with all that hair to frame her face.

"I don't know what to say."

The words tumbled out of her in a breathless rush. Her ~~eyes, the color of polished jade,~~ had ~~widened in confusion.~~

"Sa~~

HEIRS TO THE THRONE OF KYR

*Two brothers, one crown, and a royal duty
that cannot be denied...*

The desert kingdom of Kyr needs a new ruler.

Prince Kadir al-Hassan, the Eagle of Kyr:
the world's most notorious playboy.

Prince Rashid al-Hassan, the Lion of Kyr:
as dark-hearted as the desert itself.

These sheikh princes share the same blood,
but they couldn't be more different. So now there's
only one question on everyone's lips...

Who will be crowned the new desert king?

Don't miss this thrilling new duet from
Lynn Raye Harris—where duty and desire
collide against a sizzling desert landscape!

GAMBLING WITH THE CROWN

BY
LYNN RAYE HARRIS

Published in Great Britain 2014
by Mills & Boon, an imprint of Harlequin (UK) Limited,
Eton House, 18-24 Paradise Road, Richmond, Surrey, TW9 1SR

© 2014 Lynn Raye Harris

ISBN: 978 0 263 90853 4

Harlequin (UK) Limited's policy is to use papers that are natural,
renewable and recyclable products and made from wood grown in
sustainable forests. The logging and manufacturing processes conform
to the legal environmental regulations of the country of origin.

Printed and bound in Spain
by Blackprint CPI, Barcelona

USA TODAY bestselling author **Lynn Raye Harris** burst onto the scene when she won a writing contest held by Mills & Boon®. The prize was an editor for a year—but only six months later Lynn sold her first novel. A former finalist for the Romance Writers of America's Golden Heart Award, Lynn lives in Alabama with her handsome husband and two crazy cats. Her stories have been called 'exceptional and emotional', 'intense', and 'sizzling'. You can visit her at www.lynnrayeharris.com

Recent titles by the same author:

A GAME WITH ONE WINNER *(Scandal in the Spotlight)*
REVELATIONS OF THE NIGHT BEFORE
UNNOTICED AND UNTOUCHED
MARRIAGE BEHIND THE FAÇADE

Did you know these are also available as eBooks?
Visit www.millsandboon.co.uk

To my editor, Flo Nicoll, who always pushes me—
very politely—to do my best.

I complained and moaned and dragged my feet
on this one, but you were right.

PROLOGUE

THE KING OF Kyr was dying. He sat in his chair on the balcony, wrapped in a blanket—though the desert sun had not yet sunk behind the horizon and brought cooler temperatures with it—and contemplated his life.

He'd had a long reign, a good reign, but it was time to name his successor and make sure Kyr continued to thrive when he was gone. He could no longer put off calling his wayward sons home and determining which of them would be the next king.

He pushed to a standing position, unwilling to give up even a tiny bit of independence while he still had strength in his body. The cancer would win, but not today. He moved slowly but surely, making his way toward the desk in his study while a hovering servant shadowed his every move. Waiting to pick him up should he collapse.

Well, he was not collapsing. Not yet.

He had one last task to finish. And it began with two phone calls.

CHAPTER ONE

EMILY BRYANT STRAIGHTENED the severe black skirt she wore, patted the French twist she'd wedged her hair into and steadied the coffee in her hand as she faced the double doors that led to the bedroom of His Most Exalted Highness, Prince Kadir bin Zaid al-Hassan.

Outside, the sky was that special blend of salmon and purple that indicated dawn's approach. Despite the early hour, Paris was awake and rumbling on the city streets below. Soon, Kadir would be awake, too.

Just as soon as Emily knocked on the carved wooden door. She frowned and dragged in a fortifying breath. The man was impossible—and probably not alone. If this morning was anything like other mornings, she'd be stepping over lacy underwear, rumpled stockings and a couture dress lying in a heap on the floor. On one memorable occasion, a bra had dangled from the priceless Venetian glass chandelier. What city was that in?

Ah, yes, Milan.

Emily firmed her lips in what she knew was a distasteful frown—she couldn't abide messes, especially from people who should know better—and lifted her hand. Then she rapped three times.

"Prince Kadir? It's time to get up."

No matter the hour he came in the night before,

Kadir always wanted to be awakened before the sun rose in the sky. Sometimes he went back to sleep, but not before peppering her with orders and instructions about the day. And not before he drank the coffee she always brought.

More often than not, he got up. Emily had learned to relax her expression into an impassive and unimpressed mask of cool professionalism when the covers whipped back to reveal sleek tanned skin and acres of lean muscle. She'd also learned to turn her head discreetly to the side on the rare occasions when he'd failed to add clothing to his lower half before he leaped up and shrugged into his robe.

If he were any other man—if this were any other job—she'd probably be horrified. But this was Prince Kadir, and she knew what the job entailed. He'd warned her as much when he'd hired her. When he'd expressed that a man might be better suited for the job of his personal assistant, she'd assured him she was up for the task.

Therefore, she endured his quirks and his singlemindedness. If he weren't brilliant, if he didn't pay her extremely well—*extremely*—she might not have stayed as long as she had. Not to mention that getting this job straight out of college had been a coup. She still believed that if Kadir hadn't been so desperate to find someone who could put up with his shenanigans, he would never have agreed to interview her, no matter how impeccable her references.

"Come." His voice was dark and raspy with sleep on the other side of the door.

Emily opened it up and walked across the darkened room in her sensible heels. There was a time when she'd loved platforms and flash as much as the next girl, but these shoes were a whole lot more comfortable. She opened the thick damask curtains to let in the light and took his coffee over and set it on the antique bedside table.

A quick perusal of the room indicated he was alone. She breathed a sigh of relief. She did not like the woman he'd been dating recently. Lenore Bradford, fashion's latest runway darling, was not nice in general and evil to Emily in particular.

It was as if the woman was jealous, which was insane, since Kadir had never once looked at Emily as anything more than the person who ran his life and kept his calendar up-to-date. But that did not stop Lenore from shooting Emily angry looks or demanding outrageous things from her.

Like the morning Lenore had wanted chocolate croissants from a *boulangerie* halfway across Paris. Croissants she knew damn well she would barely sniff before turning to the egg-white omelet instead. Emily had fumed the whole way. Fortunately, she'd not had to do that again, because Kadir had been rather angry when he found out.

Yet another thing Lenore blamed her for. But Kadir wasn't a stupid man and he could read the address on the bag, which apparently Lenore did not try to hide when she tossed them aside as predicted.

Kadir sat up against the headboard and picked up the coffee. His dark hair was tousled and he needed to shave, but he was still one of the most attractive men she'd ever seen. Not that she was attracted to him. Of course not. He was an arrogant, entitled, brilliant jackass and she did not like men like that.

Heck, she probably wouldn't like him at all if he didn't pay her so much.

Except, dammit, that wasn't quite true. He drove her crazy with his cool confidence and certainty he was always right, but he remembered her birthday and the anniversary of the date she'd started working for him. She liked to think that meant he cared about people in his own fashion, though it was probably just that mind of his, which never forgot a fact.

But she chose to believe the former; therefore, she couldn't dislike him.

Much.

Emily flipped open the notebook she'd tucked under one arm and steadfastly ignored the sheet as it slipped down and revealed a hard, muscled chest and that damn arrow of dark hair that marched down the center of his abdomen and disappeared beneath the fabric.

"You have a seven-thirty meeting with the chairman of RAC Steel, and a phone call after that with Andrakos Shipping. There is also the real estate agent to meet with on the specs for the property and a site inspection this afternoon."

Kadir sipped the coffee and peered up at her from beneath those impossibly long lashes of his. His eyes were a clear, dark gray that snapped with intelligence.

Really, did a man so beautiful also have to be so smart?

"You are a model of efficiency as always, Miss Bryant. *Shukran jazeelan.*"

She glanced at her watch and tried to ignore the flush of pleasure rolling over her. "Breakfast is on the way up, Your Highness. And I have told the driver to be here at seven sharp."

Kadir's gaze slid over her. He was assessing her, the way he assessed everyone, but she always felt that strange little prickle that started at the back of her neck and continued down her spine like electricity dripping through a conduit.

She didn't like it. She licked her suddenly dry lips and closed the notebook. Kadir's eyes narrowed.

"If that is all, Your Highness?"

"It is."

She turned to go when a racket sounded outside the doors to the bedroom. She wasn't particularly alarmed, as Kadir traveled nowhere without armed guards, but it was unusual in the extreme. She started toward the door when Lenore Bradford burst in.

Emily drew up short. When she realized she clutched the notebook to her chest, she lowered it. Her heart thudded alarmingly. Behind Lenore, a man in a dark suit stood there like a mountain. An angry mountain, she realized.

He would have let Lenore into the suite, because she'd been here before, but he would have expected her to wait while he announced her.

Clearly, she had not done so.

"Lenore." Kadir's voice would have sounded lazy to anyone listening. But to someone who knew him, who'd worked beside him for four years, the note of danger was distinct.

Oh, Lenore. You've done it now.

Emily closed her eyes briefly and waited for the coming storm. Behind her, the blankets stirred and she knew that Kadir had risen and put on his robe. He must have flicked a hand in dismissal because the guard melted away.

"You walked out on me last night," Lenore shrilled. "It was *my* party, and you walked out."

"Perhaps I would not have done so had you not invited six reporters and a camera crew. I am not bait for your ambition, Lenore."

Lenore's pretty hands fluttered and her eyes widened. She was blonde, tall and thin, perfectly coiffed from head to foot, even at this early hour. A real looker, as Emily's dad would have said. But she wasn't very bright where Kadir was concerned. He was not the sort of man to be handled or manipulated.

Emily started for the door again, intent on getting out of the room before the fight blew into the stratosphere. Not that Kadir would tolerate much of that, but Emily didn't need to be here for it. It was personal, and while she might like to snatch Lenore bald-headed for being such a bitch, it was none of her concern.

"Stay where you are, Miss Bryant." Kadir's voice was commanding, as always, and Emily froze. "Lenore was just leaving."

The other woman's skin flushed pink. "I won't leave without discussing this, Kadir. If we are to have a relationship, we have to talk about these things. Perhaps I was wrong, but—"

"It is Prince Kadir or Your Highness," he said coolly. "And there is no relationship. There will be no relationship. Now, get out."

Every word was measured and mild, as if he could hardly be bothered to get angry. Emily almost felt a pinprick of sympathy for the other woman. Almost, but not quite.

Kadir moved past Emily until he was between her and the door. Facing Lenore. He was clad in a navy silk robe and his hair was still tousled, but he looked every inch a prince. It was hard not to admire him in these moments. Her heart swelled with a strange kind of pride that confused her.

Lenore had gone purple. "That's it? You are not even going to talk about it with me?" Kadir didn't answer as he stood there with his arms folded and gave her his best imperious stare. Emily couldn't see his face, but she knew the look. And she could see its effect on Lenore's expression.

Lenore suddenly pointed a manicured finger at Emily. "You think I don't know what's going on here? You think I don't know about your *assistant*—" she somehow made the word sound dirty, as if she'd said *whore* instead "—about how she's tried to come between us from the beginning? She wants you for herself!"

Emily opened her mouth to utter a protest, but Kadir was there first. "I don't particularly care what Miss Bryant thinks of you. It is what I think that matters. And I am finished."

He strode to her side, took her by the elbow and marched her toward the front door of his suite while she screamed at him. Then she was thrust through the door, and it closed again with a thud. Kadir turned, his face black with fury. Emily dropped her gaze and studied her shoes while her heart thrummed hard.

She had never witnessed the breakup scene before, but she knew it had played out again and again over the past four years she'd worked for him. She could almost feel sorry for the women who committed the mistake of thinking there was a future with him. He was rich, titled, wealthy and successful in his own right. Every woman he dated wanted to tame him. None of them had managed it yet.

"I am sorry you had to hear that."

Emily's head snapped up to meet his hot gaze. He'd moved closer to her and her pulse skidded with unwelcome heat. "I don't want you for myself," she blurted. Her cheeks blazed.

Great.

Kadir quirked an eyebrow. "Really? I am told I am quite delightful. How stunning to encounter a woman who does not want me."

For a moment she didn't know what to say. And then she realized he was teasing her. Emily dropped her gaze again. She needed this job and she wasn't going to do anything to jeopardize it. He might be humored this time, but she could not let it pass. "Forgive my outburst, Your Highness."

"There is nothing to forgive. Lenore was incredibly rude to you."

"It won't happen again, I assure you."

He laughed. "Oh, I think it will."

Emily could only stare at him, her pulse a drumbeat in her throat, her fingers. And then she realized he meant the scene with Lenore.

"Don't look so worried, Miss Bryant," he continued, his voice smooth as silk, hard as steel. "Lenore will not be back. But there will no doubt be others."

Emily wanted to roll her eyes. She resisted the urge. Kadir's eyebrow quirked again.

"You wish to say something?"

"Your breakfast will be here any moment."

"That is not it." His voice was a knowing murmur as his gaze dropped to her lips, back up again. Shockingly, she felt as if he'd touched her. As if he'd taken one of his golden fingers and slid it across the pad of her lips. He grinned, and her insides turned to liquid. She was not happy about it either. "Come, Emily. We've known each other for nearly four years now. You know more about my life than anyone besides me."

He'd called her Emily a handful of times. It always rattled her the way his accent slid over the syllables of her name. Like a caress. Like the touch of a lover.

As if she would know what that was like these days. It had been so long since she'd last had sex she couldn't even remember when it was. She traveled too much, moving with Kadir as he trotted the globe and built his skyscrapers. It left little time for a personal life.

Except for when they were in Chicago. Then she took time to go see her dad, to make sure he had everything he needed. Dating was hardly a blip on her radar compared to that.

"You pay me to keep your life in order, not to advise you on it."

"And yet you wanted to say something. I could see it in your expression. The way your lips pursed ever so slightly. The downward tilt of your eyebrows, the flare of your nostrils. The green fire in your eyes. I would like to know what it was."

"I prefer to keep my job." Her voice contained an edge of tartness that she couldn't quite control. *The green fire in her eyes?*

"And you shall. I give you leave to say what you wish. I'd rather not have you pop from holding it in, Miss Bryant."

Emily sighed. He wasn't going to give up until she'd spoken. If she knew anything about this man, she knew that. She'd watched him in negotiations, watched the way he closed in on his prey like a hawk, circling ever closer, until the moment he snatched them up and got precisely what he wanted, whether it was a bargain on steel, a commitment to sell only to him, incentives on a piece of land or a premium from someone who desperately wanted his company to build their new skyscraper.

"I was going to say that it was ridiculous to expect more of the same. That perhaps if you conducted your, er, affairs a little differently, they might not get to this stage."

He looked amused. Heat flared in her belly.

"And how should I conduct my affairs? I would imagine that swearing off women for good would do it. But so far as I like women—and I certainly do—there will always be some who think I am going to make them my princess. They never take it kindly when they find out it is not going to happen."

"Then perhaps you should choose women based on their intellect and not their bra size."

He burst out laughing and a prickle of something ran up her spine. It wasn't fear. It wasn't even embarrassment. Perhaps it was relief. Relief that she'd said the words after all.

"I will take your charming suggestion under advisement, I assure you."

"You did ask."

"Indeed I did." He raised his arms, stretching like a supple, sleek cat. The robe fell open to reveal the tight muscles of his abdomen—along with that damn arrow of hair again. Thankfully, he was wearing a pair of black silk boxers that were perfectly decent. Emily averted her gaze as her heart rate picked up once more. Fresh fire licked across her skin, shortened her breath.

She forced it down again, buried it beneath the mountain of decorum and duty she always lived by. She was not the sort of person to be ruled by urges. She was not the sort of person to *have* urges—not anymore. She'd worked very hard to make sure of that.

So what on earth was the matter with her today? He was devilishly attractive, but that was nothing new. She'd thought herself inoculated a long time ago. Apparently, he could still rev up her pulse under the right circumstances.

Perhaps she should make an appointment with her doctor. Her hormones were surely out of whack or something. It was the only explanation.

Kadir moved with liquid grace, sauntering back into his bedroom while Emily stood and gulped in air. He didn't close the door and she soon heard the sound of the shower. She imagined him dropping the robe, sliding the silk boxers down his lean, hard thighs—

Emily gripped her notebook hard enough to make her fingers ache. Then she smoothed her hair, straightened her clothing even though it was perfectly straight already, and went to check on Kadir's breakfast.

The day had been long and productive. Kadir sat in the limo as it moved through the brightly lit streets of Paris and rubbed a hand over the back of his neck, easing the kinks of sitting at a desk for the past few hours. He'd been going over the projections for his newest project. This office building in Paris's business district was simply the latest in a series of buildings he'd constructed over the past couple of years.

But he loved the process, loved watching the steel skeleton rise high above the city and take on a life of its own. This building wasn't as tall as some he'd built, but it was modern and sleek and efficient. The company that had hired him would be very pleased when he was finished. He prided himself upon it.

Beside him, his assistant typed away on her laptop. He slanted a glance toward her. Miss Emily Bryant was quite possibly the best assistant he'd ever had. She was eager to work, professional, and she'd taken over his life with the kind of efficiency he valued.

Nothing escaped her notice. Nothing remained undone. In spite of this morning's episode, a thousand Lenores could not ruffle her calm for long.

He'd come to look forward to her marching into his room, in whatever city they might be staying in, and standing over him in her crisp black-and-white—or sometimes navy-blue or gray—business suits and ugly shoes as she told him about his day.

Emily was blessedly uncomplicated. The only female in his life who was. Thank goodness he wasn't attracted to her, or he would no doubt ruin what was the longest relationship with a woman—unrelated to him—that he'd ever had.

He thought of her this morning, telling him to choose women based on intellect rather than bra size, and wanted to laugh again. She'd shocked and amused him at the same time. He'd asked her opinion, but that was not the answer he'd expected. Emily was always so circumspect that it hadn't crossed his mind she had anything remotely sarcastic to say.

He'd loved it because it was so unexpected from his proper assistant. That was something he almost never got in his relationships with anyone: honesty. No one wanted to disagree with a prince.

His mobile phone began to buzz. He took it from his pocket and handed it to Emily. He was too tired to deal with anyone just now. She answered with that voice of hers that sounded so young and fresh, as though she was still sixteen instead of twenty-five. Kadir closed his eyes and leaned his head back against the seat. Tonight, he would sleep the sleep of the dead. No parties, no manipulative fashion models, no distractions.

"Your Highness." Emily sounded a touch breathless. Her pale green eyes were wide as she held out the phone. "It's your father."

CHAPTER TWO

KADIR GRIPPED THE balcony's iron railing with both hands as he stared at Paris spread out below. The Eiffel Tower glowed ocher against the skyline as cars slid through the streets. He could hear laughter coming from somewhere in the hotel where he'd booked an entire floor, and a soft breeze slid across his skin, cooling him.

His father was dying. The phone call tonight played again and again in his head, filling him with so many emotions that he could hardly sort them all. He remembered a lion of a man when he was a child, a man who had both frightened and awed him. He remembered wanting to be important to that man, wanting his attention and doing nearly anything to get it.

If his father had had a favorite son, he was it. Not that that was saying much, since he'd often felt his father's belt against his skin. But Rashid had felt it more. And Kadir had been so convinced as a child that if his father was angry with Rashid, then he might be pleased with Kadir—not to mention, if his father's attention were on Rashid, Kadir would escape the harsh punishments his father meted out. So he'd encouraged his father to be angry with Rashid in any way he could.

Kadir raked a hand through his hair and thought about ordering a glass of some type of strong liquor.

But he did not drink when he was alone, so that was out of the question. It was a matter of self-discipline and he would not violate his own rule.

He picked up his phone from where he'd set it on the table and willed it to ring. He knew Rashid would call him. Because Rashid would know that Kadir had been told the news first.

When he and Rashid had been children, he'd taken shameless advantage of his father's apparently strong dislike of Rashid. When Kadir let the horses out of the stables, his father blamed Rashid. When he released his father's prized hawk, Rashid got blamed. When he accidentally poisoned his father's favorite hound—who thankfully recovered—their father had blamed Rashid for that as well.

Rashid always took the punishment stoically and without complaint. He never cried during the beatings, but he would return to their shared quarters red faced and angry. Kadir shuddered with the memories of what he'd caused Rashid to endure.

It was a wonder Rashid did not hate him. He always felt such a dark and abiding shame in his brother's presence, though Rashid did not ever speak about anything that had happened in their father's palace. It was as if, for Rashid, it did not exist.

Kadir wished it were the same for him.

He stood there for another hour in the dark, waiting and brooding. And then his phone rang and an odd combination of regret and relief surged inside him.

"I've been waiting for you," he said by way of greeting.

There was a long pause on the other end. "It is good to talk to you, too, brother."

"Rashid." He sighed. He could never say everything

he wished to say to his brother. His throat closed up whenever he thought about it.

I'm sorry I caused you so much trouble. I'm sorry for everything. And then, *Why don't you hate me?*

Instead, he said the one thing he could say. "You know I don't want the throne. I've never wanted it."

In Kyr, the throne usually passed to the eldest—but it didn't have to. The king could choose his successor from among his sons, and that was precisely what their father was proposing to do. Kadir couldn't begin to express how much this angered him.

Or worried him. He was not, in his opinion, suited to be a king. Because he did not want it. For one thing, to be king would mean being trapped for the rest of his life. For another, it would feel like the ultimate dirty trick to be played against Rashid.

"You are as qualified as I," Rashid said with that icy-cool voice of his, his emotions wrapped tight as always. To talk to Rashid was to think you were talking to an iceberg. It was only when you saw him that you realized he blazed like the desert.

"Yes, but I have a business to run. Being king means living in Kyr year-round. I am not willing."

That was the reason he could voice. The other reasons went deeper.

"And what makes you think I am?" There was a flash of heat that time. "I left Kyr years ago. And I, too, have a business."

"Oil is your business. It is also the business of Kyr."

Rashid made a noise. "He only wants the appearance of fairness, Kadir. We already know his choice."

Kadir's throat was tight. He feared the same. And yet he could not accept the throne without a fight for what he knew was right.

"He's dying. Do you really plan not to go, not to see him one last time?"

If anger had substance, then Kadir could feel the weight of his brother's anger across the distance separating them. "So he can express his disappointment in me yet again? So he can hold out the promise of Kyr and then have the satisfaction of giving it to you while I can do nothing?"

Kadir felt his brother's words like a blow. He'd done nothing to deserve Kyr and everything to drive a wedge between his father and his brother while protecting his own skin, though he had not really known the gravity of his actions at the time. Still, being a child did not excuse him.

"You don't know this is his plan."

Rashid blew out a breath and Kadir could almost hear the derision. "It has been this way since we were children. He hasn't changed. You are the one he prefers."

As if being the preferred one had made life as one of King Zaid's sons any easier. Their father did not possess a warm bone in his body.

"I am not the best man to be king. You are." He could say that without regret or shame. His particular gift was in building structures, in turning steel and glass into something beautiful and functional. He loved the challenge of it, of figuring out the math and science to support what he wanted to do.

He enjoyed his life, enjoyed being always on the move, always in demand. If he were the king of Kyr, he would not be able to do this any longer.

Oh, he could build skyscrapers in Kyr—but Kyr was not the world. And a king had many other things to tend to. He loved his country. But he felt its responsibility like a yoke, not a gift.

Rashid, however, wanted to rule. Had wanted to do so since they were boys. He'd always thought he would be the one to inherit the throne by virtue of his position as eldest—everyone had—until their father announced one day that he had not yet chosen a successor. And would not until the time came.

If King Zaid had died without choosing, the governing council would have made the choice. There had been no danger of Kyr being leaderless.

But it had always been a carrot to dangle over Rashid's head, to make him jump to the tune King Zaid wanted.

Rashid had not jumped. He'd walked out. To Kadir's knowledge, his father and Rashid had not spoken in at least ten years. Kadir maintained a distantly cordial relationship with his father, but it was not always easy to do.

"Be the better man, Rashid. Go and see a dying old man one last time. Give him what he wants and Kyr will be yours."

Rashid didn't speak for a long moment. "I will go, Kadir. But for you. Not for him. And when it turns out as I said, when you are crowned king of Kyr, do not blame me for your fate. It is not I who will have caused it."

Emily nearly jumped out of her skin when there was a knock on her door. She'd fallen asleep on the couch of her small suite. A sheaf of papers fell to the floor as she bolted to a sitting position, her heart hammering with adrenaline.

She grabbed her phone where it lay on the coffee

table. It was a few minutes after midnight. The knock sounded again and she scrambled upright, looked askance at the papers—there was no time to straighten them—and then whipped the long tangle of her hair out of her face and shoved it over her shoulders.

She'd changed into her usual sleep set—a tank top and pajama pants—which wasn't in the least presentable. But the knock was insistent and she moved toward the door once her brain kicked into gear. Something must have happened to Kadir or no one would be outside her door at this hour. If Kadir wanted her, he would call.

She whipped the door back, unconcerned about criminals—since Kadir's security had locked down the entire floor they were on—though she was careful to keep the bulk of her body behind the door.

Kadir stood on the other side, looking handsome and moody, and a wash of heat and confusion flooded her at once. Her stomach knotted even as her brain tried to work out a logical reason for his appearance at her door.

"Your Highness? Is there a problem?"

"There is indeed. I need to talk to you."

"I—I will come to your suite. Give me a few minutes to get dressed and—"

"No. There is no time for that." His hand was on her door, his big masculine body poised to enter her room. She'd worked for him for four years. She knew he was strong and big and not in the least bit soft, but she'd never quite felt the intensity of his body until this moment.

A rush of flame slid through her at the thought of facing her boss in her pajamas, but she pulled the door back and let him in. She'd seen him in less, after all. To him, meetings in various stages of undress were completely acceptable.

He came inside, all darkness and intensity and coiled strength as he paced across her floor. She could only watch as he moved like a trapped panther in her small space, her heart thrumming at his nearness and beauty.

Emily tried to smooth her hair. And then she crossed her arms when she realized she wasn't wearing a bra. Not that she was in any danger of wowing Kadir al-Hassan with her B cups, but she'd be more comfortable if she was wearing one of her suits. Fully bra-ed and covered from neck to knee.

He stopped pacing and turned to face her. If she hadn't been watching him, she wouldn't have believed the look of surprise that crossed his face. Her cheeks flamed even more and she wrapped her arms tighter around herself.

"Did you need me to draft a letter for you? Make a call to the States? It's still early there, and—"

"No."

Emily shifted from foot to foot. The papers scattered across the floor irritated her sense of order. And Kadir, a prince, standing before her in trousers and a custom-fit shirt while she was a disheveled mess in her pajamas, did not bear thinking about.

His pewter gaze slipped over her and his expression grew tight. "I have disturbed you."

"I fell asleep on the couch." God, could she be any more inane?

He moved closer to her, and she felt his presence like a wave. A giant, engulfing wave of heat and sharp masculinity. This was not her urbane, sophisticated boss standing before her. This man was a prince of the desert, a man who stood on the edge of a precipice between civilization and the wild, untamed dunes.

She gave herself a mental shake. She knew better than that. He might be an Arab male, but that didn't make him uncivilized. That was as ridiculous as saying all Americans wore cowboy hats and said yee-haw.

Kadir was a man. Just a man.

Her pulse raced even while she had the oddest sensation of her blood beating heavily in her veins. And her brain whispered back to her that Kadir al-Hassan was *not* just a man by anyone's definition.

"You are…rumpled, Miss Bryant." He said it almost wonderingly, and a flash of irritation rolled through her.

"Well, I was asleep. And you usually phone if you want something."

He shoved a hand through his hair then, and she saw that he was not quite himself. Not the cool thinker she was accustomed to dealing with.

"We are going to Kyr."

She felt the force of those words deep in her gut. In four years, he had never once gone to Kyr. If she hadn't looked it up on a map, she'd have almost thought it didn't exist. But it was there, a slice of sand on the Persian Gulf. It was oil rich, as were so many of the countries in that region, and ruled by a king. By Kadir's father.

She had never spoken to the king until today. Until he'd phoned his son while they'd been riding across Paris and Kadir had handed her his phone, as he so often did when he didn't want to deal with anyone. She could still hear that raspy voice, the note of command as he'd told her he wished to speak to his son. He had been imperious and polite all at once, though she had not fooled herself that politeness would win out should she attempt to take a message.

Kyr. My God.

It was perhaps the most foreign of any location he had ever taken her to, with the exception of Singapore and Hong Kong.

"When?"

Kadir blinked, and she wished she had her notebook. She felt professional with her notebook and pen. She also had a tablet computer, of course, but she liked the feel of the pen scratching over the paper as she made quick notes—and then she transferred them later so that she could access everything on the tablet. His calendar was there, too, but not until she'd jotted it out on paper first.

"In the morning."

Emily bit her lip. Kadir didn't take his eyes off her and she started to worry that he'd had a shock of some sort. He was not behaving like himself, that was certain.

"I will be sure to have everything ready. What time would you like me to request wheels up?"

"I have done this already." He shoved his hands into his pockets and looked around her room as if he'd never seen it before. Which, she supposed, he hadn't. "Do you perhaps have a bottle of wine? Some scotch?"

"I—um, there might be wine. Just a moment."

She went to the small refrigerator tucked beneath the cabinets on one side of the room and pulled out a bottle of white she'd been nursing. Then she took down a glass and poured some in it. But when she turned, he was behind her. He'd moved so silently she'd not heard a thing.

Or perhaps it was the way her blood beat in her ears that prevented her from hearing something so basic as a person walking across the floor. He loomed over her, so tall and vital and surprising. It jarred her to realize that without her heels, she really was much shorter than he.

She thrust the glass at him without a word.

"Please have a drink with me."

Emily turned and poured wine into another glass, thankful to have something to do that did not involve looking at Kadir. But when she pivoted again, he was still there. Still in her space, still big and dark and intense.

She thought he might move, might go over and sit on her couch, but he didn't. He simply stood there, staring at the liquid in his glass. And then he raised his gaze to hers, and she felt the blow of those eyes like a twist in her heart.

She recognized pain when she saw it. His seemed to swallow him whole, turning those clear gray eyes to the darkest slate. She had an urge to lift her palm to his cheek, to tell him it would be okay.

But that was a line she could not cross. He was her boss, though she was having a very hard time remembering it just now.

"What is the matter, Your Highness?" The words were tight in her throat, but she forced them out anyway.

His brow furrowed. And then he lifted the glass and took a deep swallow of the golden liquid. Once more, his eyes were on hers. As if she were an anchor. As if it were her alone keeping him tethered to the earth, keeping the pain from engulfing him.

"My father is dying." The words were simple, stark, and her heart squeezed into a tight ball in her chest. She knew the pain of those words, knew how they opened chasms in your soul. How they could change you.

But she also knew the bittersweet joy of finding out there was a way to save the person you loved. The worry over if there would be enough money to pay for the procedure—not that this last was a worry a king would have.

She reached for him automatically, gripped his forearm. She had never dared to touch him before, not deliberately. Not like this. The jolt of sensation buzzing through her should not have been so unexpected. But it was. Like touching a live wire and then being unable to let go.

She had to push past it, had to speak. Had to get beyond the awkwardness and confusion when he needed so much more from her than this giddy schoolgirl behavior.

"Is there nothing they can do?" Her voice came out a whisper, but he heard it. He'd been staring at her hand, at her pale fingers clasped over his golden skin, and he raised his gaze again.

Once more, the blow of those eyes threatened to steal her breath away. Her sense. For a moment, she wished she were someone else. Someone beautiful and dynamic. Someone who could interest a man like this.

But no, that was silly. She wasn't a sensual creature. She was sensible. There was no room in her life for the kind of heat and exhilaration that went along with a man like Kadir. She'd seen how women burned for him, and how they burned out too soon. That kind of heat wasn't worth the price.

She'd almost been that sort of woman once, but she'd learned that it was far better to be sensible and staid. And if she ever doubted it, she had only to think of her mother's tragic example of what could happen to a woman who followed her hedonistic tendencies too far.

"No, it's too late now. They've done everything."

He sounded almost detached and cool, but she knew

it must affect him deeply. She squeezed his arm. "I'm so sorry."

He put his hand over hers and lightning sizzled into her deepest core. In four years' time, their hands had brushed on occasion. It would have been impossible if they hadn't.

But this. This was too much, like walking out into full sunlight after having spent a year in a cave. The feelings swirling through her were too hot, too bright.

Too confusing.

Kadir was an attractive man, but she was not attracted to him. She liked lean blond men who weren't quite so tall. Quiet men. Men who didn't make her feel jumpy and achy just by touching her.

She had to force herself to meet his eyes, because to continue to stare at his hand over hers would certainly be odd. The pain was still there, but there was something else, too. Something that flared bright for a moment and was extinguished.

She'd always known that Kadir was a complicated man. But this felt as if someone had lifted the curtain to show her the gears and pulleys that ran the show.

She'd seen beneath the veneer. Beneath the walls. But only for a moment.

A moment she was not likely to forget any time soon.

"I am angry, Emily."

"I believe that is normal." She remembered being angry herself when they'd first learned that her father needed a new heart if he were going to survive. It had seemed impossible at the time—and she'd been so furious with fate—but then a heart had become available and he'd gotten his second chance.

But every moment had been agonizing. The feelings, the fear. Not everyone in her family had handled it well. Her father had survived—but the family had not.

Kadir's gaze was searching. She had to remind herself, strongly, that he was still her boss, that this breach of their usual formal relationship was a temporary thing. If she handled this wrongly, if she did what she wanted to do—which was put her arms around him and pull his head down to her shoulder while she stroked the thick softness of his hair—she would be crossing a line that could never be redrawn.

"I need something from you, Emily."

His voice was soft and mesmerizing and her stomach tied itself into a knot as she imagined what he might ask for. But then she told herself he was simply hurting and this change in their usual relationship was a temporary by-product of that. He needed someone to talk to and there was no reason why she couldn't be that someone.

"Anything I can do, Your Highness."

One corner of his sensual mouth lifted in a smile. She'd never spent a lot of time gazing at him—she was far too busy taking care of business—but she could certainly see why the women he dated seemed to melt so quickly beneath the power of his raw male beauty. His mouth begged a woman to press her own there. His hair needed a woman's fingers in it. His shoulders needed someone's arms around them. His waist needed to be surrounded by a woman's legs—

Oh, my. Emily clamped down hard on her wayward thoughts and tried to look like her usual professional self.

Which would be far easier to accomplish if she were not standing here in her pajamas with her hair a dark tangle down her back.

He put a hand on her shoulder, his fingers touching

bare flesh. She couldn't quite contain the gasp that escaped her as an arrow of flame shot through her belly, down into her deepest core. Oh, she was so going to the doctor the instant they returned to Chicago. There had to be a pill that would fix her raging hormones. She was entirely too young for this kind of wild fluctuation.

Kadir's brows drew down, his gaze searching hers. His eyes were dark, glittering slate, and she had to force herself not to shrink from the fire in them.

"First, you are going to need to call me Kadir."

Her stomach flipped. "I—I don't think that's a very good idea. You're my boss, and I prefer to keep that straight in my head. First names invite familiarity, and—"

His finger over her mouth silenced her. And burned into her. Confusion set up a drumbeat in her brain, her blood. She had no idea what was going on here, or where it would lead if she let it.

"Emily."

He said her name simply, but it had the effect of sending a wave of calm over her. She drew in a breath and waited. Whatever he was going to say, she could handle it.

His next words shattered that illusion. "I need you to marry me."

CHAPTER THREE

SHE WAS LOOKING at him as though he'd grown two extra heads. He didn't blame her, really. What he was proposing was perfectly outrageous. But after that phone call with Rashid, he couldn't stop thinking about how he wasn't going to be forced to take his brother's birthright.

He wasn't the next king of Kyr. Rashid was. And he wasn't going to allow his father to use him as a bludgeon in his personal war with Rashid. Not any longer. When he was ten, he hadn't understood. He understood now.

He was returning to Kyr because his father was dying and he believed it was important to be there. But Kadir wasn't going to make it easy for the old man to do what Rashid believed he was going to do.

And for that, Kadir needed a very unsuitable bride. A woman who would horrify his father enough that he would believe Kadir's judgment so poor he would not, under any circumstances, give the kingdom of Kyr into his keeping.

An American woman with no connections or pedigree would fit the bill nicely. If he could persuade her to act a little more like Lenore—spoiled, entitled and manipulative—it would work even better, though it was not strictly necessary. Her origins would be enough for his father and the staunchly traditional governing council.

King Zaid would turn to Rashid, regardless of their differences, and choose the son who was the only sensible choice. He would not risk his kingdom with a son who was blinded by the charms of a most unsuitable woman.

Kadir knew it was an insane plan, born of desperation, but he was determined to carry it out. Nothing else would work. His father might be petty, but he was much too proud to allow Kyr to pass into the hands of a son who showed such a decided lack of judgment.

"I...I..." Emily raised a hand to push a stray lock of hair from her face and he was once more confronted with a fact he had somehow managed to ignore for the past four years.

Emily Bryant was not quite the unattractive automaton he'd believed her to be. Her brown hair was long, thick and shiny—and very tumbled. He'd never seen it down before. She either wore it scraped up on her head or pulled back in a severe ponytail.

And now her mouth had somehow become enticing, with all that hair to frame her face.

He'd known she was not shapeless. Indeed, her suits were well-fitted and crisp, if stark in color—it was only her shoes that were ugly. Sensible shoes, he believed they were called.

She was almost boyish, with narrow shoulders and hips. But she had a waist, and her small breasts were shapelier than he'd realized beneath her suit jackets. That surprised him in ways he hadn't expected. He knew it now because he'd had a devil of a time keeping his gaze from straying to where they jutted against the thin fabric of her top.

Still, she was Emily, his PA. Not some woman he could take to his bed and discard. He needed her in his life, and at this moment he very much needed her to agree to his plan.

"I don't know what to say." The words tumbled out of her in a breathless rush. Her green eyes, usually the color of polished jade, had darkened in what he supposed was confusion. Or horror. There was always that possibility, he decided.

"Say yes."

She did the one thing he did not expect. She took a step backward, out of his space, and wrapped her arms around her body. The wineglass was still clutched in one hand and tilted precariously to the side.

Her chin dropped and he got the distinct impression she was meditating. When she looked at him again, her gaze was clear.

"Why are you asking me this? Do you need to be married for a business deal? Is there some piece of property you cannot do without and a wife would ease the way with the owner?"

He could only stare at her. She was so close to the truth it astounded him. And yet not quite.

"I need to take a wife home to Kyr."

Her brows drew down. "I don't understand."

He blew out a breath. "It is very complicated. But suffice it to say that a wife is necessary. Think of this as a promotion."

She blinked. And then she laughed. He was almost insulted.

"This is the strangest promotion I have ever heard of." She drew in air, straightened her spine. "And it's impossible, Your Highness. I cannot do what you ask."

He felt the sting of her rejection as if it were a blow. It stunned him, if he was truthful with himself. Women did not typically refuse him.

"And why is that? This is a job, Emily. The same as always."

"You will forgive me, Your Highness—"

"Kadir." He spoke sharply, but he could not seem to help it. For once, he wanted her to call him by his name. For once, he needed to know that he was more to her than a paycheck. It was beyond insane, and yet he'd not felt quite right since he'd spoken with his father earlier.

It was as if everything he'd known had flipped upside down. As if his life had started out one way this morning—a lifetime ago now—and ended up in a completely different place. He was at the bottom of a pit, trying to find a handhold to pull himself back up again before the walls caved in and crushed him.

She swallowed. He didn't think she would say it, but then she did. "Kadir." Her voice was so small, so quiet, as if she feared that saying his name would call down a bolt of lightning.

"Was that so difficult then?"

Her eyes glinted in the dimly lit room. "No."

"Good." He retreated a few steps, gave her space. He sank onto her couch, ignoring the scattered papers. "Do I pay you well, Emily?"

She moved to one of the chairs set around a small table several feet away and sank down on it as if she feared she would break it. "Yes."

"Then you can hardly object if I give you an extra year's salary once you complete the task. All you need do is pretend to be my wife."

Her eyes were wide. "Pretend? We wouldn't actually be married?"

"We would, but it won't be a real marriage. I don't want you to think I expect anything other than the pre-

tense of devotion." Because they would need to appear
ridiculously besotted with each other for this to work.

She looked doubtful. "Won't someone figure it out?"

"How? We will act our parts."

She shook her head. "No one will believe it. Just yesterday, you were with Lenore Bradford. You were probably photographed with her. And now you are marrying
me—when, tonight? After you were with Lenore at her
party last night?"

He felt the noose tightening around his neck. "I did
not say it was a perfect plan. But we will sell it, Emily."
He twisted the stem of the wineglass in his fingers.
"Besides, Kyr isn't precisely connected to the outside
world. Not in the way you would think. It is modern,
certainly. But gossip and tabloids are hardly my father's
daily reading material. If I arrive with a wife, a wife
who I am clearly crazy about, that will suffice for him."

He could see her throat work. "You want to deceive
your family?"

"Yes."

"I don't understand."

He sighed and leaned his head back, staring up at the
ceiling. She would never understand. And yet he had
to make her do so if this were to work. It went against
his nature to explain himself, but he had to acknowledge that she could just as easily turn him down if he
did not. "It's about the throne, Emily. I don't want it."

She blinked. "Why not?"

A riot of emotion twisted through him. He wanted
to lash out. To tell her it was none of her business. And
yet, if he was asking her to do this thing, it surely was
her business. He could tell her the truth without delving
into his personal reasons. His guilt. That was private.

"Because a king cannot travel the world and erect

buildings. My business will be finished. And you will be out of a job."

He didn't like pointing it out so cruelly, but what choice did he have? Because that was, ultimately, what was at stake for her. If he became king, he couldn't keep her in Kyr. He'd have an entire legion of assistants and she would not be needed. Even if he wanted her there.

There was a hierarchy in serving the royal family in Kyr, and Emily Bryant did not fit into it.

She put her forehead in her palm and slanted her gaze toward him. It was an unconsciously attractive look. A twinge of heat flared to life in his belly. He tamped it down ruthlessly. His life was upside-down, he reminded himself. He was not attracted to his very ordinary assistant. If he had been, he would never have hired her. Besides, if he hadn't found her sexually appealing in four years thus far, he wasn't going to start today.

In spite of the awareness that slid through him when she'd put her hand on his arm. In spite of the urge he'd had to bend his head and fit his mouth to hers, just to see if the sparks would continue or if it was simply the incongruity of her touching him so deliberately.

An anomaly. Stress.

"I don't like the idea of deceiving your family. Besides, I'm a terrible actress. No one would ever believe I was your wife."

Kadir allowed himself a smile. It was the kind of smile he knew usually had an effect on the women he turned it upon. "I have no doubt they will believe it. You've never yet failed at a task I've set for you. And you won't fail at this one." He leaned forward then, elbows on knees, and delivered what he hoped would be the coup de grâce. "You are the only person I can trust, Emily. The only one who will not fail me. I need you."

* * *

Emily's insides were spinning and churning as though she'd taken a ride on a merry-go-round. It didn't help that Kadir looked at her so seriously. Or that he was specifically asking for her help. How could she refuse him?

And how could she go through with it? No one would ever believe that she—plain, ordinary Emily—was Kadir's chosen bride. The whole world would see through the deception.

And she'd be mortified when they did. People would laugh and point fingers. She would be noticed, and not in a good way.

It was impossible.

Yet, he looked at her with those gorgeous dark eyes and serious expression and she wanted to do whatever he asked. She closed her eyes, swallowed. It was more than that, though.

One year's salary.

With that kind of money, she could finish paying her father's hospital bills and start to put money in the bank for his long-term care. He still lived in the house she'd grown up in, but it was an older house that always needed repairs of one type or another. He tried to do things himself, but it was too much for one frail man.

Anger scoured through her then. Her mother should have been there with him. *Would* have been there with him if she weren't selfish and self-serving. If her focus on herself hadn't led her down a self-destructive path and ended in a twist of steel on a dark highway.

When Emily's father had needed his wife the most, when he'd gotten too sick to work and couldn't keep buying her clothes and vacations and cars, she'd said she was too young to be someone's caretaker. And then she'd run off with another man.

Emily experienced the same cold wash of helpless fury and despair she always did when she thought of her mother. Emily had been heading down the same path, in some ways. She'd loved flashy clothes, loved dressing up and being the center of attention. She'd spent hours at the salon, hours shopping with her girlfriends and hours discussing men. She'd had boyfriends, more than one at a time, because they lavished her with attention and gifts. And that had made her feel special.

But everything changed when her mother deserted them. Emily had realized what a self-destructive road she was traveling when there was no one left to take care of her father except for her. And now Kadir was handing her an opportunity to finally pay off her father's bills, maybe move him to a retirement community in Florida. He'd always wanted to go to where it was warm. Maybe live in a golfing community and play a few rounds.

If she could do that, it would mean the world to him. And to her, because then she wouldn't worry so much about him living in the windy, bitterly cold Chicago winters.

"How would this work?" Her voice sounded rusty, as if she hadn't used it in ages and her vocal cords didn't want to let the words go.

Kadir sighed and bowed his head for a brief moment. She wanted to tell him that she had not yet agreed, so he shouldn't get all relieved and everything—but they both knew she was going to. It was simply too good an opportunity to pass up.

No matter how it terrified her.

"My attorneys will draw up the paperwork. We will sign it. That is all that is required in Kyr—a legal marriage document, with both signatures affixed. We can have a ceremony in Kyr, if you like, but the documents will suffice."

She couldn't imagine standing at an altar—or wherever one did these things in Kyr—and pledging everlasting love to this man. To her boss.

No matter how fake it would be.

"I don't need a ceremony."

He tipped his head, as if he'd known she would say that. "Then there will not be one."

She clasped her hands in her lap, twisted them together. It was incongruous to be discussing marriage with her boss while in her pajamas in Paris, but that's precisely what she was doing. How surreal.

"Will there be other paperwork? A prenuptial agreement? A contract detailing the terms of our arrangement?"

"Do you require either of those things?"

She could only blink at him. "It seems prudent, don't you think? What if I decide I like being a princess so much that I refuse to divorce you and then ask for half your assets when you insist? Or what if you become unhappy with my performance and decide not to pay me?"

He laughed and she let the sound drip down her spine, warming her though she did not want it to.

"You are delightful, Emily. If I don't tell you that enough, I am remiss." He got to his feet then and she stood, too, more out of habit than anything. "I will have those documents done as well, if it makes you feel better."

She sucked in a fortifying breath. "I haven't said yes yet."

"But you will."

Heat rolled through her. She would, but she didn't like how easily he could read her. Or maybe it wasn't that at all. Maybe he just expected her to obey. Because she always had before.

"How can you be so certain? This is far different than ordering me to make phone calls or type up a new proposal."

He came closer to her and she forced herself to remain where she was. She would not duck away like a frightened kitten. Then he put his warm hands on her shoulders and she felt as if she'd been struck by lightning again.

"I need you, Emily. More than I've ever needed you before. And I think you will say yes because you've worked for me for four years now and you are good at what you do. You won't want to walk away when I need you. It's a challenge, and you like challenges."

She could only stare up at him, her insides clenching and rolling as his touch made things jump inside her. Things that hadn't jumped in a good long while.

"I—I have conditions," she managed.

His brows drew down, but he didn't look angry. "Conditions?"

She swallowed. *It's for the money. For my dad.* "For this to work, you can't order me to do things. The moment we sign the documents, I am no longer your employee."

His gaze slipped to her mouth, and she thought her knees might refuse to hold her a moment longer. But then he looked at her again, an expression of curiosity and bemusement on his handsome face. "Do you want to be more, Emily? Oddly, I find I might enjoy such a notion—"

"No." She cut him off, and immediately wanted to gasp. She had never done such a thing before. He was gazing at her steadily so she hurried on. "Partners. We will be business partners."

It was the only way she could do this. If she continued to think of herself as his employee, she would never manage the deception. Because she knew what happened when bosses and employees crossed the line. And she was too professional to do so, even if it was only an arrangement. For her own peace of mind, she had to separate those parts of her life.

"Fine." He didn't seem angry in the least.

Her heart throbbed painfully at what she was about to say. "Then I'll do it. I'll marry you."

Kadir seemed to relax slightly, as if he'd believed for a moment she might actually refuse him. His hands slid almost sensuously down her arms, left a trail of flame in their wake. Her skin prickled and tingled. She wanted to shrug away, to get out of his grasp—and she wanted to move closer at the same time.

"There are only two things left to do in order to seal this deal." His voice was like silk and she shivered in response.

His hands dropped away then, but before she could breathe a sigh of relief, he reached up to cup her neck. Then he drew her forward as her heart hammered. Her feet moved as if he was the one in control of them rather than her.

"Wh-what?" She cursed herself for sounding nervous—but he was touching her, and apparently that made her light-headed.

"First I have to fire you," he murmured, his gaze focusing on her mouth as she came in contact with the broad wall of his chest. Her hands went up automatically, rested on the soft cotton of his shirt. He was hard and warm beneath the fabric. She knew he went to the gym, and she knew what his body looked like beneath the cotton. Firm, tanned, beautiful.

No, she told herself. *You don't care. You haven't cared in four years.*

She had to focus, had to concentrate on what he was saying rather than on what he was doing. She could not lose her perspective here. "What's the other thing?"

His eyes glittered and one corner of his mouth lifted in what could only be termed a self-satisfied smile. "I have to kiss you, Emily."

CHAPTER FOUR

SHOCK RIPPLED THROUGH her like a wave. It was quickly followed by a pang of heat and longing that nearly took her breath away. Kadir pulled her more firmly against his body, and then his head dipped toward hers. She closed her eyes automatically, her heart hammering so hard she was going to be dizzy.

Kadir was going to kiss her. Her boss for the past four years, the man she'd served across continents and time zones without one single moment of inappropriateness, was about to kiss her.

Just like he'd kissed Lenore Bradford yesterday and a million other women before her. Emily had watched the revolving door of his life for far too long. She'd seen the women come and go. She'd walked many of them to the door herself as they clutched their handbags. Half the time with their wadded-up panty hose trailing from their purses as they took the walk of shame.

She'd witnessed it and, if she was honest with herself, she'd been utterly judgmental. What kind of idiot woman got herself involved with a playboy sheikh? Oh, she knew what they all thought. What they hoped. That they were *the* one. The one he would marry and make into his princess.

Sure, some of them just wanted sex, the same as he

did. And that was fine. She didn't pity those women, the ones who knew what they wanted and what they were getting.

The majority, however, were the other kind. The dreamers and schemers and hopefuls.

And she was not about to become one of them.

Emily shoved against his chest. His grip immediately eased and she stepped backward, out of his grasp. Her chest rose and fell as if she'd run a marathon. She wrapped her arms around herself, embarrassed at the effect he was having, and moved farther away.

Her wineglass was waiting on the table, so she picked it up and took a gulp. Then she faced him again. He looked oddly on edge, like a tiger waiting to pounce.

"No kissing," she said hoarsely.

"I'm afraid that is a condition I cannot accept." He sounded so cool, so calm, as if touching her hadn't meant a thing to him. Which, of course, it hadn't. His pulse wasn't racing like hers. His breath wasn't a struggle. She was simply another female to him.

"You have to."

He shook his head, his eyes glittering dangerously. "Impossible, Emily. I can hardly be besotted with a wife I never kiss, now can I? Besides, you have already agreed. You cannot change the terms of the agreement afterward. That is bad business."

She clutched the wineglass like a lifeline. She knew he was right, but dammit, why hadn't she thought of it before? Why hadn't she made it a condition?

Because it's stupid, that's why. Because he's paying you to be his wife, and husbands kiss their wives.

"Fine, you can kiss me. But only in public. Only when it's necessary for the illusion. No touching in private. No kissing either."

His eyebrow quirked. "Are you that afraid of me, Emily? Worried about what kissing me will do to you?"

Heat flared beneath her skin. "With all due respect, Your Highness, you really need to get over yourself. It's not professional, is all I mean. I'm your partner, not your lover."

"So no mixing business and pleasure, I take it?" He sounded amused, and it irritated her. Was there really nothing she could say that bothered this man? That got to him the way he was getting to her?

Maybe she should have been more blunt with him much sooner. But she'd always tried to be cool and professional and detached. She hadn't wanted camaraderie with him. She'd wanted nothing but her job and her paycheck and the satisfaction of performing her duties better than anyone he'd ever employed before.

She'd wanted to be indispensable to him—and she'd wanted to be the one he trusted with his business life. She hadn't wanted to kiss him or touch him or, heaven forbid, lie naked in a bed with him.

To do that would be like picking up a treasure map, pointing right to the place that said "Here Be Dragons," and saying, "This is where I want to go."

No, not going there. Not ever.

"Precisely." She tried to sound like her usual cool self, but there was a hint of hot color in her voice. She could hear it vibrating. She didn't like it.

He shoved his hands into his pockets. It was such a casual move, and yet he looked no less intense—or delicious—than a moment ago.

Stop.

"All right, we'll do it your way. For now. No touching unless necessary for public consumption. Which, by the way, includes my staff and anyone in the palace in Kyr. I expect this to work, Emily."

The tightness in her chest seemed to ease a bit now that she knew he wasn't going to try and tug her into his arms again. "I know that. And I will do my best."

"You better do more than that." He moved toward her with an easy grace that made her think of leopards slinking across the savannah. He stopped before her, hands still in pockets, intense gray eyes roving over her face. "Because if you don't, Miss Bryant, everything is going to change. And then you will be out of a job for real."

When dawn came, Emily didn't know what to do with herself. She started to get up and get dressed as usual, prepared to go to Kadir's suite and wake him as always—but then she remembered that he'd fired her. That she was no longer his employee.

Temporarily, of course. But as much as she wanted to adhere to her usual routines because they gave her comfort, she had to play a different role in his life right now. She'd spent the last several years learning to be sensible and efficient and now she was at loose ends. It was strange.

So, instead, she lay in bed and tried to go back to sleep. It didn't work, in spite of the way she'd tossed and turned last night. She hadn't slept because she'd been remembering Kadir standing in her room, looking so lost and alone and handsome, and asking her to marry him. And then he'd taken her in his arms and tried to kiss her.

Her heart did a little skip-and-slip thing every time she thought of that moment when she'd closed her eyes and felt him dipping down to press his mouth against hers.

But she'd panicked and pushed him away and now she couldn't stop wondering what she'd missed. If she'd made a mistake.

No. She had not made a mistake. Kissing him would have been a mistake. Allowing him to sweep her off her feet the way he'd done to countless women over the past four years would have been a mistake.

Asserting herself, asserting her independence and setting up parameters was not a mistake. It was good business. Kadir would respect her for it. And in the end, if this worked the way he hoped and he did not inherit the throne of Kyr, she would slide back into her role as his PA. So long as this arrangement stayed strictly business between them—including any touching or kissing that was required for the role—there would be no awkwardness later on.

Still, her stomach twisted in such a way that belied her thoughts. But she refused to let her fears get the upper hand. This was a business arrangement, albeit an uncharacteristic one. And she would do her part without fear or complaint.

Still, she worried about the way he'd been last night. He'd proposed this crazy idea, and she'd agreed, but what must he truly be feeling inside? His father was dying. She remembered that moment when he'd told her. He'd said he was angry and her heart had gone out to him. She'd known him for too long to be unaffected by his pain.

And yes, she'd agreed to help him. For the money. But also for him.

Emily threw back the covers and launched herself out of bed. She took a shower and dressed in her usual business attire—because it was all she had besides a few pairs of jeans and casual shirts—and slipped on her low heels. And then, because she wasn't quite sure what else to do with her hair when she felt as though she was dressed for work, she pulled it back in a severe ponytail.

Her cell phone rang just as she finished putting on lip gloss. One glance at the screen and her stomach started doing backflips. Emily took a deep breath and willed the butterflies away. It was ridiculous to get worked up, especially since Kadir called her often and it had never bothered her before.

"Yes," she said, hoping she sounded cool and calm.

"I need you to come to my suite, Emily. The lawyers are here."

She swallowed. Part of her had begun to hope it had all been a dream. "All right. I'll be there in just a few minutes."

She ended the call and took another look at herself in the mirror. All the color had drained from her face until she looked pale and ghostly. God, she was really going to do this. She was going to walk into Kadir's suite and marry him.

For the first time, a little stab of distress caught her by surprise. She should have worn something different from her usual attire. Something a bride would be happy to say she'd gotten wed in. Something special.

Emily closed her eyes. Except this was merely an arrangement and it wasn't supposed to be special. What was the matter with her? Why did she care what she wore when all she was going to do was sign some papers?

Papers that would change her life, albeit for a short time. She really, really hoped that Kadir knew what he was doing. It was a crazy plan, but she'd agreed to it. Too late to back out now.

She took one last look in the mirror, smoothed her ponytail and went to meet her fate.

Kadir waited impatiently for Emily to arrive. He paced back and forth in the living room of his suite while the lawyers arranged the documents on a nearby table. The sun had glided above the horizon an hour ago now, and the Paris sky was clear and blue, with wisps of feathery clouds sailing across it.

A perfect day to get married.

He tried not to shudder at the notion. Marriage was not something he'd ever intended to enter into lightly, yet here he was. It wasn't that he didn't believe in marriage, or didn't believe in falling in love—it's just that he'd never actually seen it work in his own life. His father had many wives and he didn't seem emotionally attached to any of them.

Kadir's mother had been the favorite wife before she died, but she had been desperately unhappy. Something Kadir hadn't realized until he'd gotten older.

The door to his suite opened and Emily sailed inside, looking as cool and businesslike as ever. For some reason, that irritated him. Her hair was scraped back from her face, as always, and she wore a navy-blue suit with a coral shirt—the only bright spot of color on her—and those same damn ugly shoes as always. Low heel, boxy toe, matte black.

He'd never cared one way or the other before, but now he found that he despised those shoes. Utterly. She needed new ones, and soon.

"Are you coming to take notes or to get married?"

Her green gaze snapped to him and he had the sudden thought that she wasn't quite as cool as she'd like to appear. That knowledge made him relax, though only marginally.

She ran a hand over her jacket, as if smoothing an imaginary wrinkle. One thing he knew about Emily Bryant was that she didn't dare to allow wrinkles. She was always crisp and organized, and she looked just as if she was marching in for a day's work rather than about to sign the documents that would make her his wife.

He was almost insulted she'd not made more effort. But then he chided himself. What did he care? This was about presenting his father with an unsuitable bride and declaring himself unfit for the throne, not about her current clothing or enthusiasm. So long as she appeared enthused in Kyr, he could care less what she did here.

Or so he told himself.

"I'm not carrying a notebook." Her words were pointed. And completely unnecessary since he could quite clearly see she was not holding her characteristic pad and pen.

He swept a hand toward the table where the lawyers sat. "Then if you will come this way, Miss Bryant, we shall take care of business."

She nodded once, firmly, but he didn't miss the way she bit her lip or the tremor in her fingers as she tugged her jacket hem. His buttoned-up PA wasn't as calm as she pretended to be.

Good, because he wasn't very calm either. His entire future depended on this performance. Not for the first time, he wondered if he should have gone after Lenore, made up with her and asked her to do it instead. She would have agreed for the notoriety, and she would have horrified his father into naming Rashid his successor within hours of her arrival in Kyr.

And then Kadir would have divorced her. In spite of Emily's remark last night about what happened if she didn't want to divorce him, that truly wasn't possible in Kyr. All he had to do was have the decree drawn up, sign it, and it was done. He had no fear that any woman could trap him permanently.

Emily took a seat at the table and Kadir sat beside her. He was far more aware of her than he wanted to be, but that was because she fairly vibrated with energy. One foot bounced against the other as she sat with her ankles crossed, tapping it impatiently.

Or nervously.

He had a sudden urge to reach over and pull the elastic from her hair, to see it fall down over her shoulders in a silky cloud of rich chocolate. He blinked and stiffened. Really, that was not in the least bit like him. He liked a certain type of woman, and Emily Bryant was not it. She wasn't beautiful. She didn't have blade-thin cheekbones or the kind of face a camera loved. She was ordinary.

And yet his blood hummed at her nearness. He told himself it was everything to do with his plan and nothing to do with her. Once this was done, his father would choose the correct son for the throne. That was certainly enough to make his blood buzz with excitement.

He should feel guilty for dragging Emily into this, knowing what it would be like for her in Kyr, but he was desperate. And he would compensate her handsomely for the trouble.

Kadir reached for the documents and slid them toward her. "It is all fairly straightforward. Here is the paper you required, which spells out the task you are performing and your payment." He lifted a paper. "And here is the prenuptial agreement. It states that you will get nothing of my estate or business beyond what we've agreed to in the contract."

She took them both and read them over. They were both very plain documents, as he had only had them drawn up because she'd insisted, and did not consist of pages and pages of legalese.

She picked up the pen lying near her right hand and quickly signed first one and then the other. Kadir did the same and one of the lawyers took the documents and slid them into a briefcase. The other lawyer handed the next set of documents to Kadir and he set them on the table between him and Emily.

"This is the marriage contract. We have only to sign it, and we are legally wed under the laws of Kyr."

She let out a small sigh and he slanted a look her way. She was chewing the end of the pen and she slipped it out of her mouth almost guiltily.

"It seems so sterile," she said. "Almost unreal."

"I assure you it is very real. The moment we both sign and Daoud here affixes the seal, we are married."

"It's not very romantic, is it?"

He frowned at her. "I was not aware you wanted romantic."

Her head snapped up, her green gaze colliding with his. "Oh, no, of course not. That's not what I mean. I just think of the couples who get married this way and how disappointing it must be."

"Most of them hold a ceremony after, if they are doing it for romantic reasons. When you are raised this way, it is not a disappointment. You're thinking of American girls and their white weddings, with all the flowers and pomp." He frowned. "Which seem to go disastrously wrong fairly often, if the television is to be believed."

Her lips fell open as she stared at him, and he found himself wanting to slide his fingers across them, to see if they were as soft as they looked. But then she laughed. And she kept laughing, until a tear slid from one eye and she clutched her stomach.

Kadir couldn't help but laugh with her, though he wasn't quite sure why. She wasn't taking this seriously, and he should be stern with her.

But he couldn't be. He liked the sound of her laugh. He didn't know that he'd ever heard it before. It was light and soft and yet so very, very infectious at the same time. Even the lawyers were laughing, though not as much. And none of them, save Emily, knew what they were laughing at.

"Emily," he finally said, trying to be stern. She looked at him and then dissolved into another fit of giggles. Her mascara was ruined, but he didn't think she'd like him to point that out.

Instead, he jerked his chin at the man nearest the box of tissues. A second later, he thrust the box at Emily. She took several.

"I'm so sorry," she said, gulping between giggles. "Really. I'll be fine in a minute. Honestly."

"I'm afraid I don't know what is so funny. Do you care to share it with us?"

She sucked in several deep breaths and wiped her eyes with the tissues. Finally, she seemed to have it under control. "I'm so sorry. But, well, it's you." She clutched her arm around her belly, as if willing herself not to laugh again. But the corners of her mouth lifted in a smile she couldn't quite control. A smile that quavered at the corners.

Kadir thought that he ought to be insulted, but he was having a hard time figuring out precisely why. Not to mention seeing her this way—lit up from the inside instead of calm and controlled and professional—was somehow addictive in a way he hadn't expected.

"And what have I done to amuse you so much, *habibti?*"

She sucked in another breath, let out a giggle, swallowed hard. "You. *Bridezillas.*" She waved the tissue back and forth, as if fanning herself. It was a very inadequate fan. "I never knew that a prince such as you would—" She took a deep breath, let it out again. Closed her eyes. He could tell she was biting her lip. When she spoke again, her voice shook. With laughter, he realized. "Watch a show about insane brides wreaking havoc on their grooms and everyone connected with their wedding. It's just so, so…"

"Amusing?"

She closed her eyes. "Oh, God, yes." She waved a hand at him without looking at him. "Because you're so, well, you. And I just can't picture you with the remote and a bag of potato chips, settling in for the latest episode."

"Emily."

She cracked open one eye. "Yes?"

"I think you are blowing this out of proportion. I may have seen something while in a hotel room once. I also read the newspapers. The American fascination with the perfect wedding has not escaped my notice. And what I am saying is that couples in my country don't feel that same need. They have ceremonies. They throw parties—or their families throw them—but this is how it begins. At a table, with marriage documents."

She focused on the papers. "Yes, of course. I didn't

mean to insult anyone. It's just not what I expected I would do someday."

"I am not insulted. Daoud is not insulted. Philippe is French—and he is most certainly not insulted."

Her eyes were warmer than he'd ever seen them. So green, like fresh fields in summer. She made him think of sunshine and long afternoons with a book and a bottle of wine—things he'd not done in a very long time. Since he'd started Hassan Construction, he'd had no time for anything but work and the kind of erotic play that happened with the opposite sex.

He did not mind that so much, usually.

"Good." She put her hand on the marriage documents and took a deep breath. "Do I sign first, or do you?"

"The bride signs first." The words were tight in his throat for some reason.

Emily picked up her pen and wrote her name quickly. Then she sighed and pushed the papers toward him. Kadir signed and handed everything to Daoud, who affixed the official seal of Kyr. Then both lawyers stood and bowed to Kadir and Emily both before taking their leave.

Soon, the room was empty but for the two of them.

Kadir had stood to see the lawyers out, but Emily was still sitting in her chair and looking somewhat shell-shocked. He sat down beside her, took her hand in his. She gasped softly and stared down at their clasped hands. A current of warmth slid through him.

"They bowed to me," she said. "I didn't expect that."

"You are a princess of Kyr now. Emily al-Hassan, Her Royal Highness and Beloved of the Eagle of Kyr."

She blinked. "Eagle?"

He rubbed his thumb inside her palm. Her skin was

soft, warm. And he enjoyed the slight tremors vibrating through her. As a man, he knew it was not a fear response. It was a response to him, to his skin against hers.

It was a response he understood. A response he could work with. If necessary, he would seduce her into perfect compliance with his plan. A real performance instead of a fake one. A part of him rather liked that idea.

"I am the Eagle of Kyr." He shrugged. "My brother is the Lion of Kyr, and my father is the Great Protector. This is tradition. Perhaps you find it silly, like the wedding documents."

For the first time, he was aware of how foreign this must all seem to her. How very strange. He could tell her that her culture was just as strange to him sometimes, but he didn't think that would help matters at all.

She looked stricken, and he wanted to kick himself. "I don't think that at all. I really don't."

He squeezed her hand. "I know. This is all a bit overwhelming, I imagine. Yesterday you were my PA. Today you are my wife."

Her head dropped, her gaze falling to her lap. "It is somewhat stunning, I have to admit."

He tipped her chin up with a finger, forced her to look at him. She seemed younger than her twenty-five years at that moment. A bit lost, maybe. He didn't like the guilt that pierced him at that look on her face.

"It will be fine, Emily. We'll get through these next few days and then everything will go back to normal."

"Yes, of course we will. I won't disappoint you, Your Highness. You can count on me."

"I know that. And it's Kadir, Emily. It's important you call me by my name from now on."

She pulled in a breath. "Kadir."

He smiled to reassure her. "That was not so difficult, was it?"

"It will take some getting used to."

He let his fingers glide down the column of her neck, more out of curiosity than anything. Her eyes widened—and then she pushed her chair back, out of his reach.

"We're alone." She sounded almost scandalized.

There was a stirring deep inside him, a primal urge to capture and claim. He would not act upon it, however. It was simply a reaction to her moving away. Her flight response triggered his male desire to pursue.

"I am well aware of this, Emily."

"Our agreement was no touching in private."

Anger flared inside him. "And yet there is the danger you will call me something other than Kadir, or that you will flinch when I dare to caress your cheek. If you do this in Kyr, we will fail."

"I won't, Your—Kadir." He didn't miss the way she ground her jaw at her near miss. Determination shone from her pretty eyes as she lifted her chin and met his gaze almost defiantly. "You can count on me. Like always."

He stood and ranged toward her, watched the glide of her throat as she swallowed. But she didn't move again, didn't try to escape, and he felt a hot burst of admiration for her. There was his fearless PA. That was the woman he could count on, with his very life if necessary.

She tilted her head back to meet his gaze when he stopped in front of her. Close enough to feel her heat, to smell her perfume. Closer than he would have done had she still been merely his PA.

She did not flinch as he let his gaze wander over

her face, did not speak as she waited. Finally, he met her eyes again. His voice, when he spoke, was soft and contemplative.

"I hope so, *habibti*. For both our sakes."

CHAPTER FIVE

"ARE YOU READY for this?"

Emily swung her head toward Kadir. They were in the back of a limousine that had taken them from the airport in Milan to the fashion district in the city's center. She was still reeling over the short plane ride when, for the first time ever, she'd been the object of countless bows and *Your Highness*es. It was a far cry from how she usually traveled with Kadir. Then, she would sit in her own section of the plane and work on whatever needed working on. Sometimes, if he needed her for something, she joined him.

This time, she'd sat down right next to him and been served by the same people she used to joke with on their usual flights. Everyone had looked at her as though she'd forgotten to put on clothes or something. It had been far more uncomfortable than she'd expected it to be and she was still processing it.

"I doubt it," she said. She'd argued at first, when Kadir had told her they were stopping over in Milan in order to buy her a wardrobe, but she'd lost. Spectacularly.

She could still see his handsome face creased in a frown as he'd told her that her clothing was simply not suitable for a princess. Her shoes, he'd informed her, were the ugliest things he'd ever seen.

She'd been angry more than anything, but also a little embarrassed. So she'd informed him that walking around behind him on job sites and in the various offices he traveled to was not conducive to wearing six-inch heels.

"Yes, but my wife will wear them," he'd told her imperiously.

And now they were here, in Milan, for a shopping trip that she dreaded. It wasn't that she didn't like pretty clothes. She did. But she'd put away that side of herself a long time ago. And she'd never been tempted to bring it out again. She'd seen the damage that kind of life did.

She'd been a magpie like her mother, seeking beautiful things, beautiful experiences. She'd never realized how selfish she'd become until her father got sick and she'd wanted to run away, too. It had horrified her so much that she'd vowed to change her ways.

Her mother had run away, but Emily had not. She would not. She'd put away the glitz and glam and gotten serious. And now here she was, working for Kadir and dressing like a professional. She was happier. Calmer. Settled.

Safe.

Kadir was frowning at her. "It's important that you look the part, Emily."

It wasn't the first time he'd told her this. "I know."

"I need you to be more like Lenore."

A hot wave of anger flooded her. She would never look like Lenore Bradford in a million years. "Perhaps you should have asked Lenore then," she snapped.

His eyes widened only marginally. And then they narrowed again while her heart beat hotly. Well, dammit, she was tired of hearing about Lenore and how gorgeous she was and how Emily needed to be more like her.

"I did not ask Lenore." His voice was icy. "I asked you. And you agreed, I might add. So stop pouting and start doing your part."

"I'm not pouting, Kadir." At least it was getting easier to say his name, probably because she was so furious with him half the time. "I know what you want and I'll do my best to make it happen. Though I still don't understand *why* you don't just tell your father you don't want to be king. Surely he would understand that. It's not like you're his only choice."

His teeth ground together. His gray eyes flashed hot and sharp, but she wasn't intimidated. Not this time. What was he going to do? Fire her for good?

Maybe later, but not before he got what he wanted. She suppressed a shiver and refused to look away from that mesmerizing stare.

"It does not work that way."

"Why not? Is there a law against saying you don't want to be king?"

"Emily." His voice was a growl. "This is not something I wish to talk about. Leave it."

She folded her arms over her chest and turned to look at the window. "Fine. But stop harassing me. I'm sure Lenore would have been perfect for what you want, but then you'd be stuck with a woman who wanted you as a husband for real. And no matter what agreement she signed, she'd probably try to talk you out of it. Or screw you out of it, I imagine."

He muttered something in Arabic that she thought might be a curse.

"What?" she demanded. "Am I wrong?"

There was a wild, hot current swimming in her veins. A feeling that made her bold, made her fling herself against the forbidden gates of Kadir's life in utter fury. She realized with a start that it must be four long years of pent-up frustration with this man finally gaining a voice. Four years in which she'd done her job, kept her mouth shut and watched him be a complete ass to the women who rotated through his life.

Well, he'd freed her now, and she wasn't going to waste a moment of it.

Which, a small part of her tried to say, was career suicide. How would they ever go back to the way things were before? They'd been married for less than six hours, and already she was forgetting how to behave like his PA.

"You are not wrong."

The air between them grew thick, so thick she wanted to roll down the window and gulp in the Milanese air. But she was frozen in place while he speared her with those intense eyes. The Eagle of Kyr. *My God.*

Something was happening, something she couldn't quite figure out. But then he took a deep breath and shifted in his seat, his hot gaze facing front again, his jaw set in a hard line.

"Your opinion of me is showing, *habibti.* Make sure it doesn't happen in public."

"I don't know what you're talking about. I'm simply pointing out the truth."

His eyes were bright as he swung around to look at her. "That I am shallow? That I date women for, what was it, their bra sizes?"

"I didn't say that." She closed her eyes briefly. "This time, I mean. I was only pointing out what you already know to be true. Lenore would have been a perfectly unsuitable wife, but she wouldn't have given up the position so easily. Not when it made her a princess and gave her something she could lord over everyone else in her life."

"But what you really want to know is what I saw in her in the first place. What I saw in any of them." His voice was low and intense.

"That is none of my business." She knew she sounded prim, and her cheeks flamed. Because he was right, she did want to know. The women he dated were beautiful, but most of them were schemers and, well, groupies of one sort or another. None of them had wanted to see beneath his masks. They'd wanted the prince, the billionaire, the sheikh. They had not wanted the man. Didn't that bother him? At least a little?

"Mostly, it was sex." He went on as if she'd not spoken. "Sometimes, it was companionship. I am not a robot, Emily. I like the warmth of another person next to me. I get lonely, like anyone."

Her heart was beating hard now, throbbing in her throat. She'd never thought of him as lonely. Never. He always had people around him. He had friends in every city they visited, and he had women he took to his bed. How could he be lonely?

But she knew how. She knew because she'd been lonely, too. The loneliest she'd ever felt was in a crowded room. Emptiness was not filled by crowds of people. She was pretty sure it wasn't filled by sex either, though it had been a long time since she'd experimented with that.

"I'm sorry." Her voice was paper-thin. How had this conversation taken a turn like this? It had started out being one thing and ended up as something else entirely. Something that made her heart ache and tears press hard against the backs of her eyes.

How did he do this to her? How did he take her from murderously angry to aching in the space of only a few moments?

"And what about you, Emily? Do you get lonely? You cannot have much of a personal life working for me."

Her blood felt thick in her veins. Like syrup on a winter's day. Except she was hot with embarrassment as well. Why had she not seen this coming? Had she really thought she could snap and push him and come away unscathed?

"My life is fine."

He leaned back in the seat then, draped an arm on the armrest between them. His fingers dangled off the end, tapped some imaginary beat in the air. A slow, lazy beat. When she lifted her eyes to his, he was watching her with a hooded expression. Then he picked up that hand and slid his index finger across his lower lip, as if he was thinking.

Didn't matter why, since the effect of the gesture was currently what had her beginning to panic. Something bloomed deep inside her, in her core. Some hot, dark feeling that wanted very much to be allowed to blossom into a fuller, darker emotion.

Emily bit the inside of her lip. After all these years, after how ruthless she'd been with herself, her mother was beginning to creep out. That carnal, needy woman who wanted fun and adventure and licentious couplings with incredibly hot men.

She put her hands in her lap and clasped them together. She'd worked too hard. Too long. She was nothing like her mother. Sensuality might lurk within her, but she would not give in to that side of her nature ever again. It was under her control. Kadir al-Hassan was *not* going to reduce her to the kind of woman who would do absolutely anything for one night in his bed. Not ever.

"Is it?" he finally asked.

"Of course. I'm perfectly happy." And yet she did miss human connection sometimes. Not that she would admit that to him. She would not give him fuel for the fire he was building.

His expression grew sultry. "All those nights when I sent you away, when another woman joined me in my bed—did you think of me, Emily?"

She gasped. "Of course not—"

"Did you want to be the one beneath me?"

"No!"

He leaned toward her then, his eyes intense. "Did you lie in your lonely bed, touching yourself, pretending it was me?"

She couldn't speak as pain bloomed deep in her soul. Not because she'd done what he said—but a dark part of her had wanted to. And he knew it. Somehow, he knew it. The pain spread through her in waves, knotted her belly, clenched her throat tight. She was choking, choking on rage and hate and—and longing, damn him.

Tears gathered in the corners of her eyes then. She turned her head and dashed them away. She'd known he was ruthless in business. She'd known he always won. She hadn't known he was cruel. She hadn't known the depths to which he could make her sink in despair, or the fathoms-deep hatred she could feel for him.

She wanted to speak, wanted to metaphorically slap him down. Wanted to deflate his ego—and, yes, his penis—all in one well-timed verbal blow. She wanted to decimate him.

And she couldn't find the words. Nothing would

dredge itself up from the recesses of her brain. Nothing happened. Nothing except a long, taut silence that seemed to stretch forever but was in reality only a few moments.

The car came to a stop. Emily didn't care if they'd reached their destination or if they were only stopped at a traffic light. She yanked the handle and the door swung open, spilling in light and hot air and the sounds of Milan.

Kadir reached for her, but she slipped his grip and stumbled onto the street. Then she ran. She could hear Kadir shout at her, but she kept going, losing herself in the crowd, running blindly as the tears she'd been holding in finally spilled over and rushed down her cheeks.

CHAPTER SIX

KADIR CURSED HIMSELF as he ran down the crowded street after her. What the hell had he been thinking? Why had he been so needlessly vicious? Emily was his assistant, the closest thing he had to a friend in some respects, and she was doing him a favor.

And he had ripped into her as though she was just another gold-digging social climber. Worse, as though he hated her. He'd shredded her as if it was nothing, and that shamed him. What kind of man was he? What kind of man attacked those weaker than himself?

He couldn't say why he'd done it, except that he'd been irritated when she'd asked him so plainly why he didn't just tell his father what he wanted. As if it was that easy. He wasn't accustomed to explaining himself to anyone, and here she was, making what she thought was a simple suggestion when it was far more difficult than anything she could imagine.

And then she'd thrown Lenore in his face. All right, so he'd mentioned Lenore first—but then she'd kept on going, her contempt so evident. He'd simply had too much. He'd told her something personal, admitted his loneliness to her—and then he'd felt the need to lash out, to make her pay in kind.

He should have stopped much sooner than he did.

He should have stopped when she'd gotten the point. But of course he hadn't. Driven by his need to win, to crush, to control, he'd kept going until he'd hurt her.

And now he was chasing her down the street, angry with himself, and wondering how in the hell such a simple idea had gotten so complicated. She was supposed to be his wife, the woman he couldn't live without, the woman he would not give up for a throne. It was supposed to be simple.

But it wasn't.

He thought he might have lost her, but then he saw her as the crowd parted in front of him. She was walking now, her body hunched over as she hugged herself. Her ponytail bounced as she hurried along. She was moving fast, but he was faster. He closed the distance between them until he was right behind her.

She kept walking—and then she seemed to stiffen, as if she sensed a change in the air, before she halted abruptly. He took a step back as she swung around to face him. Her brows were drawn down in a furious expression. Her mascara had run again, and tears streaked her cheeks.

Something twisted inside him.

"Forgive me," he said simply. It was odd to be apologizing, and yet here he was, doing just that. It wasn't something he did often and the words were rusty.

She drew in a deep breath and straightened even more. Then she moved into his space. Poked him in the chest. It was not what he expected and he stepped back in surprise.

She closed the distance, poked him again. "Listen to me, you Neanderthal, and listen good. I do not want you. I have never wanted you. You're a handsome man, and you damn well know it. And you're used to being irresistible to women. Well, not to me." She sucked in a breath, her voice quavering as she continued. "I will not be talked to like I'm some kind of whore you pay to grace your bed. I'm your business partner, you hear me? Nothing more, nothing less. You might frighten a CEO into doing things your way, but you would never cross a personal line to do it."

He felt as if she'd slapped him across the face. Several times. Which, no doubt, he deserved.

"No, I would not. You are correct."

Her face scrunched up even more. She was, for some reason, attractive as hell when she was angry. He'd never seen Miss Emily Bryant in a fit of temper before. Well, not before today. And not like this.

He was oddly stimulated by her anger. He could feel the air crackle between them and he wondered how it had never happened before. How he'd never felt that subtle shift of electricity, that hum and buzz of ozone. Had she really kept all this under wraps for four years? Or had he never paid attention before?

"I want the money, Kadir. Nothing more. I agreed because of that. Not because of you."

It was always the money, with any woman in his life. That was a language he understood. Still, he felt a prick of anger in his gut. "The money. Of course."

She stood there, trembling—and then her hands dropped to her sides and her expression, while still angry, softened into something a notch below cyclone level.

"You really are too full of yourself," she said. "Not every woman wants a ride on your magic mattress."

He felt his eyebrows climb his forehead. "Magic mattress?"

She shrugged. A soft flush stained her cheeks. "Whatever you call your love nest, Kadir. Not every woman on this planet wants a turn. It would be healthier for you if you'd stop thinking so."

He suddenly wanted to laugh. And tug her into his arms so he could feel that bright fire radiating from her as it sizzled into his pores. It was a shock to realize that he wanted her. That he actually wanted to see what her mouth felt like beneath his. To peel away her staid suit and bare her lithe body for his eyes only. He wanted to run his fingers over her skin, wanted to see if she was as soft as he thought. As responsive.

He stood there in the hot sunshine and stared down at his former PA, now his wife, and felt the shift of his axis.

In the space of a few hours, he'd become utterly intrigued. For four years, he'd never noticed her as a woman—well, not often, anyway—but now he couldn't seem to shove her back into the box she belonged in. It didn't matter that she was wearing her conservative suit and ugly shoes, that her hair was pulled back or that tiny black rivulets stained her cheeks.

There was a commotion in the crowd and Kadir turned. His bodyguards were making their way toward him. Irritation flashed into him, not because they were doing their jobs, but because they were drawing attention to him and Emily.

People stopped to look—and then someone whipped out a cell phone and began to snap photos.

"We need to go," he told Emily. "We are being noticed."

She started to turn, but he grabbed her hand and tugged her into the curve of his body. She didn't pull away when he put his arm around her and started down the sidewalk in the direction they had come. She was so small in his grip, so warm. It was a shock to feel so much of her against him. Heat surged into him.

And confusion.

He hurried her toward a shop as his bodyguards took care of crowd control. Another moment and they were inside the couture house he'd been bringing her to in the first place.

"Your Highness," a man said as he came forward. "We are so glad you have come to us. Everything is ready."

"She must be glamorous and insanely beautiful," Kadir said, dragging his attention back to the matter at hand. He could not afford to feel softness for her right now. "Make her clothing tasteful but sexy."

Emily gasped. "I will not—"

"It is not up for discussion, Emily. You have agreed to it."

Her jaw worked and her eyes flashed cold fury. "You have no idea how much I'm beginning to regret that."

He only stared at her. "Too late, *habibti*. You are mine now."

He whirled and stalked out of the shop before she could say another word. And before he could drag her into his arms and silence her rebellious mouth with his own.

Emily could have chewed nails and spit fire. She was horribly, incredibly angry. With Kadir. With herself. But she had agreed to this insane scheme and now she had no choice but to endure the transformation currently taking place.

She looked at herself in the mirror, at her sleek hair, cut and styled and looking like mahogany silk. Her eyes were rimmed in dark eyeliner and there was a smudge of shadow in the crease. Her lashes had been curled and lengthened with mascara, her lips were a sultry red pout, and her dress was the most gorgeous shade of purple jersey that clung to all her curves. On her feet were tall snakeskin Louboutins with the signature red heel.

She'd endured endless fittings, the mechanical snick-snick-snick of sewing machines as seamstresses worked frantically to tailor the clothing and the ministrations of a makeup artist and hairstylist until finally Guido stood back and pronounced her fit for public viewing.

"His Most Exalted Highness is waiting in the outer room," Guido said.

"Wonderful." Emily gritted her teeth. She was going to have to practice being happy with her arrogant boss-turned-temporary-husband. No better time than the present.

Just thinking of Kadir caused her insides to clench. He made her so angry. He also made her itch to slide her palms over his chest while arching her body into his. That was a new development and one she did not appreciate whatsoever.

"You are a perfect princess, Your Highness," Guido said, smiling and bowing as she picked up the buttery-soft leather handbag he'd selected to go with her outfit. Emily wanted to tell him not to bow, but she stopped herself. This was a performance, and she most definitely was a princess. For now.

She glanced at herself again and swallowed. Her mother stared back at her from beneath the sultry makeup and curve-hugging clothing and Emily wanted to scream. She'd worked too hard to bury that sensual creature that lurked inside her and now it was staring back at her, mocking her.

Just because I look like you, she wanted to say, *doesn't mean I am you.*

Guido escorted Emily to the outer room, where Kadir was waiting. He looked up when she entered. His eyes seemed to widen and she told herself not to be pleased at that. The flare of feminine vanity she felt was not welcome. Oh, how she used to preen when a man looked at her with appreciation. She would not do so now.

Kadir's gaze skimmed over her slowly. And then his mouth curved in a smile that made her heart skip a beat. "You look amazing, Emily."

Heat seared into her. "Thank you." Because what else did you say to something like that?

She felt self-conscious more than anything, because now everyone was looking at her in ways they never had before. She'd found it easier to blend into the background, to be unobtrusive. Her job required that of her.

Guido snapped his fingers and a pair of smartly dressed saleswomen appeared with boxes and bags.

"These will see her through the first couple of days," he told Kadir. "The rest will be delivered to Kyr immediately upon completion."

"Grazie," Kadir said. "As always, you have pleased me greatly."

A sharp feeling sliced into her then. She remembered now why Guido's name was familiar to her. She'd been so distracted by everything today that she hadn't dwelled too much on why. But she had seen his name on bills. For shoes, clothing, jewels, handbags and silk scarves.

Of course she had. She wanted to put her hand to her temple and rub, but she didn't. What did she care if Kadir was buying her clothing at the same place he had bought things for his lovers?

Kadir might be a player of the worst sort, but one of the things he had never done was make Emily buy gifts for his ladies. He took care of that himself—and now she knew how. He picked up the phone and called Guido.

Emily smiled and thanked Guido and his staff personally, and then Kadir ushered her out the door and into the waiting limousine while a man in a dark suit and headset stood beside the car door, looking quietly lethal.

Once they were inside, the bodyguards seated in this car and the one following, the driver pulled into traffic and began the return trip to the airport.

Emily fixed her gaze on the passing city and tried not to look at Kadir. But she knew he was looking at her. In fact, he hadn't stopped since they'd gotten into the car. Her skin prickled with awareness that she tried to squash down again.

She did not need to be aware of Kadir. Not like that.

Finally, when her nerves were stretched to the breaking point, she whipped her gaze to his. "Is something wrong? Am I not being unsuitable enough for you?"

Kadir looked all dark and handsome and broody in his corner. He somehow managed to appear supremely relaxed and completely tense all at once. The tension was in his eyes rather than in his body.

"You are perfectly unsuitable. I am quite pleased thus far."

She ran her fingers over the fabric of her dress and stomped on the tendril of panic unwinding in her belly. "Well, that's a relief."

She couldn't help the bite of temper in her voice. Or the sarcasm.

"You have changed, Emily."

"You aren't used to seeing me with my hair down." She waved a hand over her body. "Or dressed like this."

"That is not what I'm talking about."

She looked at him, her pulse thrumming, her ears growing warm. "Isn't it?"

He shook his head slowly. "Not at all." His eyes narrowed. "I am not quite accustomed to this side of you. The side that—how do you say it?—sasses me."

She sniffed. "You wanted a wife, not an employee. A wife would not, I hope, take your pronouncements as law. She would state her opinions, even were they contrary to yours."

"And you have done a fine job of this. Even when there were no witnesses and therefore no need."

"No need? Kadir, you'd mow a girl down if she didn't let you know she wasn't going to take it."

One eyebrow lifted imperiously. "Surely I am not so callous as all that."

Emily leaned back on the seat and tried to appear casual. Was he really that clueless about his tendencies to overwhelm?

"You're intense, Kadir. You take over a room when you walk into it. You pull people to you, and you get what you want from them. I've seen it again and again. And the women you seduce? They don't stand a chance."

"Are you certain? You are speaking from observation, not experience."

Her mouth went dry. She licked her lips nervously. It was as if he were offering to show her, though he had not said any such thing. "I don't see how that changes anything."

His gaze was hooded and her heart performed a slow *thump-thump-thump*.

"Perhaps it does. Perhaps, if I were to seduce you, you would get what *you* want, Emily. Perhaps it would be a mutually beneficial arrangement instead of the one-sided venture you envision it to be."

Heat blossomed in her belly, slid into her bones, turned her into rubber. He wasn't actually offering, she told herself. He was simply trying to control her. Still, she couldn't move without wobbling. She didn't dare to move.

"And yet we will never know." She had to force the words out, but she was proud they didn't quaver. "Because that is not part of our deal."

"Yet deals can be amended."

Emily swallowed. The air in the car was suddenly thick and hot, and she wanted desperately to bend over and stick her face right in the air-conditioning vent. To pull some cold air into her lungs while she tried to find her equilibrium again.

She knew how to handle herself with Prince Kadir al-Hassan, her boss. She had no real clue how to deal with Kadir the man. With him, she was completely out of her element. It was as though she'd been riding a pony tied to a lead line and now someone had stuck her on top of a racehorse and told her she was about to ride in the Kentucky Derby.

The only defense she had was the truth. "If you want me to be at my best, you really need to stop. We aren't at war, Kadir. There doesn't need to be a victor."

He snorted. "And what I am trying to tell you is that you have a rather warped idea about seduction. It's not a win-or-lose game."

Yet it was for her. At least where he was concerned.

Because if she ever crossed that line, if she ever slept with him, then her career at Hassan Construction was over. She couldn't slip back into her role as his PA if that happened. Not only that, but sleeping with him would make her the sort of woman she was determined not to be. Giving in to the sensual side of her nature with a man like Kadir? Utterly destructive.

Emily drew in a breath, tried to instill herself with calm energy rather than the chaotic emotions whipping through her. And then she figured out what was happening between them. The answer popped into her head with such clarity that she was surprised she hadn't realized it before.

Kadir wasn't serious. He was prodding her because she'd argued with him. He was taking the conversation as far as he could with the goal of shutting down her protests. She'd seen him do it in negotiations a hundred times. She'd seen him take the most unwilling landowner and turn them into an enthusiastic seller by the end of the day.

He conquered people. And he was intent on conquering her, simply to prove he could. Not with sex or seduction, but with words.

Relieved, Emily smiled at him. "Whatever you say."

His gray eyes glittered hot as he seemed to go very still. "Is that an invitation, Emily?"

"Not at all. It's an admission you're right. That I have absolutely no idea what I'm talking about. I've misjudged you, and I apologize. I'm sure the women you seduce are perfectly, ecstatically happy right up until the moment you dump them. So can we please talk about something else now?"

"But I find this conversation so fascinating."

"Of course you do. It's about you." She studied her

newly manicured nails—that was something she had to get used to, since she kept them neat and trimmed and never wore polish. "You are, of course, fascinating and fabulous. But I give in, you are correct in everything you say, and now we can move on."

He leaned toward her then, and it took everything she had not to press herself into the door in an effort to keep distance between them.

"Sassing me isn't working, Emily. If anything, it's having the opposite effect of what you want."

Emily tried to laugh. It didn't come out sounding very much like a laugh, but she decided to pretend it was anyway. "I'm sure I don't know what you mean. I'm not aiming for any particular effect. I just refuse to argue with you another moment."

His gaze slid over her until she tingled as if he'd actually touched her. "Do I need to spell it out for you, *habibti?* Or would you like a demonstration?"

Emily swallowed. "It's all fun and games with you, isn't it?"

He actually looked offended. "You think this is a game?"

Her chest was tight. But that's because Kadir suddenly seemed bigger than life in the small space of the limo. It was like walking into a closet and finding a tiger on a very loose chain.

And this tiger was about to break the chain and pounce.

"What else could it be?" She had to force her voice to work, yet she still sounded wheezy, as if she'd sucked in too much air.

Dangerous. The word whispered through the air around her, caressed her skin, slipped between her ribs and into her chest to grip her heart. Kadir was very dangerous, and not in that usual impersonal way he was when she'd observed him taking down an opponent. This was deeply personal and very intense.

And it was all directed at her. Her tongue grew thick and her breath short.

He reached over and threaded his hand into the hair at her nape, very deliberately, and pulled her gently toward him. "What else indeed?"

CHAPTER SEVEN

"WE HAVE A deal!" Her voice came out as a squeak and Kadir stopped, his gray eyes darkening as he stared down at her. They were inches apart now, and she could feel the heat rolling from his body, the whisper of his breath across her lips.

Her heart slammed against her ribs and she started to see spots.

But Kadir let her go abruptly and she wilted back against the seat, sucking in a deep breath and trying not to shake. When she glanced over at him, he was looking out the window. Oddly, a wave of regret buffeted her.

The tension in his shoulders was evident and she found herself wanting to reach out and soothe him. Which was completely contrary to the way she'd just reacted. What was the matter with her? Why was she so damn hot and cold around him?

Because he was Kadir, that's why. Because she'd watched him seduce women for the past four years. She knew he was good at it—and she knew she couldn't be one of those women. She was afraid she would like it too much. She was afraid of losing control.

"Yes," he said, not turning around, his voice utterly cool. "We have a deal. And I will honor it."

She didn't know how he managed it, but he suddenly

made her feel as if she'd wronged him. Emily put a hand
to her head. Everything was wrong. Backward. Upside-
down. Why'd Lenore have to be so spectacularly stupid
so quickly? If not for that little scene yesterday morning, Emily would be riding along in the other car while
Kadir and his new wife sat in this one. It wouldn't be
her playing this role and trying so desperately not to
get lost in it, but Lenore Bradford, a woman who'd already been sleeping with Kadir and wouldn't act like
a timid virgin whenever he made the slightest motion
toward her.

And yet the thought of Lenore in Kadir's arms made
Emily's stomach twist in a way it had not only yesterday. She didn't like Lenore, certainly. But she didn't
care who Kadir slept with. She never had.

Really?

Emily gritted her teeth together. She did *not* care.
Everything was backward and confusing, that's all. She
did not want him, even though he seemed to have the
ability to make her heart pump and her body ache in
spite of her belief otherwise.

It was sensual deprivation, nothing more. She hadn't
had sex in so long she'd forgotten what it was like.

Emily stared out her window for the remainder of
the trip. Soon they were boarding Kadir's jet. It would
take roughly six hours to reach Kyr, and Emily did not
know what she was going to do with herself for the du-
ration of the journey.

Always in the past, she had worked on something
for Kadir. And then she ate and slept and worked some
more, depending on the length of the flight. This time,
she followed Kadir up the jet bridge and onto the plane
with nothing more than a chic handbag and a magazine
she'd picked up on their trip through the airport.

She felt…useless. Like a decoration instead of a professional career woman. She hated that feeling so much. It was contrary to everything she'd worked so hard for.

She also felt seriously out of place. Kadir's flight attendants—two women on this particular trip—stared at her with jaws hanging open when she walked into the cabin. She'd spent time chatting with them on previous trips, and though they'd treated her with a strange deference from Paris to Milan, this time they openly stared.

Emily felt the heat of a blush as she took her seat beside Kadir. It had been so long since she'd been the center of anyone's attention that it felt odd to be there now. She buckled herself in and closed her eyes. Beside her, she was acutely aware of Kadir as he settled in. The seats were big and roomy, with plenty of space, but she still felt as if she was too close to him. She could feel his heat, smell his scent—French-milled soap and man, no cologne for Kadir—and nothing she did could make it go away.

They were soon airborne, and one of the flight attendants came to serve drinks. Emily asked for mineral water, like always, and stared at the pages of the magazine without really seeing them.

"You haven't turned a page in twenty minutes."

She looked up, found Kadir watching her with those too-knowing eyes. "I'm thinking."

"I can imagine." He didn't sound especially friendly, but he didn't sound angry either. A good sign.

"I don't know what to expect in Kyr. You haven't told me anything."

"I don't know that anything I say can prepare you, Emily. I am a prince, and Kyr is my country. It's not the same as when we travel and I meet with clients. Outside of Kyr, I am a wealthy man with a title. In Kyr, I am royalty, with all the pomp that entails. Does this make sense to you?"

"I think so. You're telling me that the deference you receive outside Kyr is nothing like what you will experience once there."

A ghost of a smile crossed his mouth. *Sensual mouth, kissable mouth.* Emily tightened her grip on the water. She was not going to think of Kadir's mouth.

"I think you mean *we*, Emily. You are my princess."

"I'm beginning to think you've dragged me into something I'm not prepared for."

He inclined his head only slightly. "Perhaps I have. But I have no doubt you can handle it, my love."

She started to protest, to tell him not to say such things to her, but one of the attendants drifted by and she knew he'd used the endearment for her benefit.

She waited until the woman was out of earshot. "I think I need a raise. After, I mean."

"Maybe you do. But let us get through this first. There is still the chance we will fail, and then I will be the king of Kyr."

And she would be out of a job.

He looked at her hard and her pulse thumped. "We have to sell this, Emily. I need you to exude sexiness, and I need you to be passionate for me."

She wanted to fold her arms and glare at him. She settled for lifting her chin. "I'll do the best I can with what I have."

He sighed. "I did not mean to suggest you had to work at being sexy. You clearly do not—which interests me very much, by the way. Why did you hide this side of yourself from me?"

"I wasn't hiding anything. You're just blind unless a woman puts on a tight dress and makeup."

His eyes glittered. "Perhaps I am," he said without apology. "And now that you've got sexy down, I need you to be passionate. For me. Can you do that, Emily?"

Emily felt a rush of heat beneath her skin. "I said I'd try. I assume you don't want me to crawl beneath the table at dinner and minister to your needs?"

He looked shocked. And then he looked intense. She'd thrown it out there because she was irritated, but she now realized it had been the wrong thing to say. It put an image in her head—and most certainly in his—that was incredibly arousing.

"Perhaps you can save that for when we are alone." His voice was a low growl that stroked over her skin.

She waved a hand breezily, though her body sizzled with fresh heat. "I doubt that, but thank you for clearing it up. No public sex then."

"Another time."

He was silent for a long moment but she didn't dare to look at him. She didn't want to see what was going on in those eyes.

"There is something else you need to know," he said. "There will be those who are not happy I've married you, which was of course the goal. But do not be surprised if you are treated less than kindly by some."

Her stomach hollowed. "I should have asked for more money."

"Perhaps you should have. But it is too late now. We have a deal, remember?"

It was night when they arrived in Kyr, but two things struck Emily at once. First, when Kadir emerged from the back of the plane, where he'd gone shortly before they landed, he was wearing the white desert robes of his people and the dark headdress with the golden coils holding it in place. His face was all that was visible in the frame of the headdress, but it had a startling effect on her.

Emily swallowed, her mouth utterly dry. She had never seen Kadir in desert garb. His home base for the last four years had been Chicago, and they'd traveled the globe building his skyscrapers. But they'd never come to Kyr. Indeed, when she thought back on it, the few times he'd come to the Middle East at all had been during her time off. Always a quick trip, never anything he needed her for.

Oh, she'd seen his picture in native clothing before, certainly. She'd recognized that beautiful, aristocratic face and his piercing eyes scrutinizing her from the headdress.

But the real thing was a completely different experience. Kadir was tall and commanding and regal—and the desert robes made him seem even more so.

She felt underdressed and puny next to him. Panic set in. This was not going to work. No one in his or her right mind would believe Kadir had chosen her for his wife—plain Emily Bryant who cleaned up nicely but was nothing compared to the beautiful women he usually dated.

The second thing that struck her—aside from the heat of the night air—was the delegation waiting at the bottom of the stairs. Men garbed in desert robes, waiting as a group. She was accustomed to walking out of airports, discreetly following Kadir, while cameras flashed and popped into the air.

There were no cameras here. Only hard desert nomads. Emily chided herself the instant she thought it. Kyr had industry, and people did not live in tents on the edge of the harshest deserts. Some did, certainly, but most people had houses and apartments in the major cities. These were their traditional robes, but that did not make them nomads.

Kadir stood at the top of the stairs and spread his hands wide. He said something in Arabic to the gathered men. Emily stood off to the side, out of view of the men, but where she could see them from the open door.

Her heart throbbed and her palms were sweaty. Her beautiful plum dress felt like a sack now, and she wished for her comfortable shoes to walk down those stairs in. Her legs were shaking so much she didn't know how she'd manage it in high heels. Her hair was too thick and heavy, and she wished she could pull it up, off her neck and into her familiar ponytail.

She was lost in her thoughts, worrying her lower lip between her teeth, when Kadir stopped speaking. There was silence for a long moment, and then she looked up and realized he held out his hand to her.

"It's time," he said. "Are you ready for this, *habibti?*"

"Do I have a choice?" She'd wanted to sound brave and defiant, but her voice was barely more than a squeak.

The beauty of his smile hit her like a one-two punch. How had she never fully realized the power of Kadir? How had she spent four years with him and never seen *this?*

"It will be fine. You only have to appear to be madly in love with me. Just follow my lead."

Emily took a deep breath and put her hand in his. A current of electricity buzzed up her arm, into her heart, spread through her limbs until she was almost calm.

Appear madly in love with him? How could she do anything else but? How could any woman?

He pulled her to his side and wrapped an arm tight

around her. He was so close, so *right there,* and her pulse was doing crazy things in response. His smile was almost mocking.

He slid his free hand into her hair, cupped her nape like before. And this time, this time when he lowered his head, she did not stop him, though her heart knocked against her chest like a frightened rabbit. His mouth settled over hers and a shock rippled through her body, slid straight into her core and set up a throbbing response that craved his touch.

She made a noise—she knew she did—but what kind of noise she would never know. Because Kadir caressed the skin of her collarbone, glided his fingers up her throat, cupped her chin and tilted her head back.

And then his tongue slipped between her lips, stroked against her own—and she was lost.

He did not mean to kiss her quite like this. It was supposed to be a sweet kiss for the people observing them. A kiss to show he'd brought home a wife of whom he was enamored. To show he was serious.

A sweet kiss for his new wife. Not this incredibly hot, shocking, erotic tangling of tongues that had him ready to devour her. *This is Emily,* he reminded himself. *Emily.*

Yes, yes.

Emily. Something inside him responded as if it recognized her. Recognized the fit and feel of her mouth against his.

She was lush, his PA, and sweeter than he could have imagined possible. Something about her drove him perfectly insane with the kind of need he didn't recall feeling in ages—not since he'd been a young man learning his body and how it responded to a woman's touch.

She made him feel that eager, that green.

But no, that could not be right. He was thirty years old. He'd had his share of lovers over the years, but he was not jaded. Surely someone else had excited him this much. Had made him feel this, well, new.

He just couldn't recall it right this moment. And he had to cease this demonstration, before it turned into something that would embarrass them both. Already, he'd lost control of his ability to regulate his body's response.

Which was going to be quite obvious in another few seconds.

Reluctantly, he dragged his mouth from hers. Heard her intake of breath, her shocked gasp when she realized what had just happened. Her eyes fluttered open and for a moment he saw everything in them.

Lust, confusion, need, pain—so many emotions crossed those lovely eyes before she locked them down tight and pressed her lips together. Her fingers were still clutched in his robes. He thought she might let him go too quickly, might give away the game—but she didn't. Not Emily. No, she let him go softly, smoothed her fingers over his chest, her gaze dropping from his as she did so.

The shy, desperately-in-love bride. By Allah, he was proud of her for it, even if it wasn't quite the response he'd been looking for. He'd wanted her bolder and more passionate, but this first reaction was perfect.

She was amazing, his Emily. And beautiful. That had certainly been a surprise.

Guido's people had not turned her into someone else. They'd simply showcased the beautiful body she already had, highlighted her features—her cat's eyes and her lush chocolate hair. Not to mention those lips he'd just kissed. He'd never seen them in anything but a serious expression—maybe the occasional smile—but like this? Moist and swollen from the pressure of his mouth on hers? So enticing, like the sweetest honey?

How had he managed to ignore her charms for four years?

"Can you walk down the stairs?" he asked, because he had to say something. Something normal, regardless that his heart pounded in his chest and he could still feel the heat of that kiss down to his toes.

She glanced down the steep stairwell. "I'll do my best."

He took her hand in his, gripped it tight. "I'll hold you, Emily. I won't let you fall."

She smiled then, but it wavered at the corners, and he knew she was feeling overwhelmed. Guilt pierced him. He'd dragged her into this out of desperation, and now he wasn't sure it had been the right thing to do. Still, it was done, and he couldn't turn back now.

"I know you won't."

"Do you trust me?" he asked suddenly.

Because, he realized with a start, he wanted *something* about this to be real. He was back in Kyr after a long absence, and the father who'd filled his childhood with such confusing emotion was dying. The metaphorical ground—the ground he'd taken for granted, no doubt—was being ripped out from under him.

And he wanted something—someone—to hold on to. Something in his life that made sense. Just for now. Just this once.

She squeezed his hand. It was a light touch, tentative. But it was something. "I've trusted you for four years, Kadir. I'll trust you awhile longer."

He lifted her hand to his mouth, pressed a kiss to the

back of it without breaking eye contact. He didn't miss the shiver that rippled through her, or the answering shudder deep inside him.

The next few days in Kyr would be interesting indeed.

CHAPTER EIGHT

"THIS CANNOT BE happening," Emily muttered to herself as she turned around in the palatial room she'd been shown to. The floors and ceiling were tiled in the most beautiful gold-and-blue mosaic.

The walls were plain white, but the color wasn't stark in this setting. It was soothing and somewhat necessary after the ornateness of the tile. There was a living room with a sunken area that contained low-slung couches with lots of colorful cushions, and a television glided up from where it was hidden in a cabinet.

The bathroom was larger than her father's house in Chicago. There was a tub recessed into the floor and ringed with marble columns, and a shower tucked into one end of the room. There were also acres of mirrors and a dressing room that contained the clothing Kadir had bought for her in Milan.

But it was not *her* room. It was hers and Kadir's. They were sharing a room. Because that's what a husband and wife did.

How had she not seen this coming? Surely Kadir had known it—and he'd not warned her. Maybe he hadn't wanted her to freak out.

She thought back to that moment on the jet when he'd kissed her in front of everyone, and her body flooded with a fresh wave of heat. She'd been utterly lost in his embrace. She'd forgotten her name. Where she was. What was happening.

She'd forgotten it was *an act*. And that horrified her. Emily put her hands on her hot cheeks and breathed deeply.

He is Prince Kadir al-Hassan. He is a playboy. You've worked for him for four years, and you've lost count of the number of women he's woken up with.

She sucked in another breath.

No, you have not lost count. You never kept track! Because you damn well don't care!

That's right. She didn't care. He was Kadir, her boss, and all she cared about was her paycheck. Which was why she was doing this now. After the kiss on the plane, they'd descended the stairs and stood on the red carpet on the tarmac while Kadir spoke endlessly with the men waiting there.

They'd come up to him individually, bowed and then spoke in low tones while he listened and nodded. She'd felt so out of place, but she'd been unable to do anything except stand at his side. Under normal circumstances, she would have her notebook and be awaiting his orders.

But these were not normal circumstances—and her feet had been beginning to hurt. It was night, thankfully, so at least the desert was not sweltering. After what seemed to be an hour, they'd finally moved toward the limousine that awaited them. Kadir had set her inside and then climbed in beside her. A palace official took up residence in the seat across from them, notebook in hand, and spoke with Kadir all the way to the royal palace in the center of the city.

At one point during the ride, when Emily was staring out the window at the city and the palm trees, Kadir took her hand in his. She'd jumped and he'd squeezed lightly, as if warning her. She'd relaxed only a fraction, finally daring a look at his profile as he continued to speak to the man riding with them.

The beauty of Kadir stunned her in ways it had not only a day ago. She thought she'd been accustomed to how utterly stunning he was, inoculated even, but now that he touched her so sensually, she discovered she was not quite as immune as she'd always believed. He was getting under her skin and she did not like it.

For once, she was glad she didn't understand Arabic, because she would have been unable to concentrate on it anyway. Kadir's thumb rolled inside her palm, stroking softly. She felt as if he were stroking other, more sensitive places on her body. Every glide of his thumb set up an answering throb deep in the heart of her, until she was on edge and ready to jerk her hand from his grip regardless of their audience. Because, if she did not, she would melt against him and beg for more.

Thankfully, they'd arrived at the palace then. When they'd gotten out of the car, he'd hugged her close and kissed her forehead before giving her into the care of the servant who'd shown her to this room. She knew he'd only done it for their audience, but the touch of his mouth on her skin was disconcerting nevertheless. She'd been thinking about everything that had happened since she'd signed the marriage documents—and then the baggage had arrived. That was when she realized they were sharing a room.

Her anxiety levels had gone through the roof then.

She was still pacing and wondering how to fix this mistake when Kadir walked into the room. He looked… angry. That was a surprise. She blinked, but before she could say anything he speared her with a stormy look.

"You are upset with the sleeping arrangements, no doubt."

Emily drew in a breath. It suddenly didn't seem like the time. And yet he already knew what was bothering her. She gestured at the bed. "There is only one."

He stalked toward her, his expression not softening in the least. "Yes, because husbands usually sleep with their wives, even in Kyr." His gaze dropped over her body as he came to a halt. Her skin prickled with heat. "Perhaps especially in Kyr."

She tried not to let the sensual tone in his voice get to her.

"This isn't a public place, Kadir."

His eyes glittered hot. "No, it is not. But if I ask for another room, or another bed to be brought into this one, there will be questions. And I am not willing to answer those questions, *habibti*. It defeats the purpose of our agreement."

She turned her head to look at the bed. At least it wasn't small. Maybe if they put pillows down the center, it would work. It would *have* to work.

"Fine. But you stay on your side."

"If you insist."

She lifted her chin at the mocking note in his voice. "I hope you plan to wear more than you usually do."

One dark eyebrow arched. "I don't know, Emily. The desert is very hot. And one does not wear flannel pajamas to bed in Kyr."

Heat flared inside her at the thought of him naked. Beside her.

Oh, dear.

That simply could not happen. She'd seen him without clothing, yes—but not often and only briefly. The barest flash of male flesh before he robed himself.

This, however, was different. She drew herself up.

"Yes, but this is a palace, not the desert. And I saw a thermostat, which tells me there is air-conditioning. Turn it down and put on some clothes before you come to bed."

Kadir laughed, but the sound was low and sensual and her belly tightened into a knot. "I will consider it."

"You need to do more than consider it."

He looked amused, which was a nice change from when he'd entered the room. She wanted to ask him what was wrong, but she felt as if it would be prying to do so. She was still getting accustomed to this shift in their relationship, however temporary, and she didn't want to cross any deeply personal lines.

"Afraid of losing control, sweet Emily?"

"What? No!" She put her hands to her blazing cheeks and shook her head, her heart thumping in response. "You're outrageous, Kadir."

He walked over and took her wrists gently in his, pulled her hands away from her face. She felt as if she was going to hyperventilate, and he stood there so calm and in control that she almost envied him. Yes, damn him, control was precisely what she was afraid of losing.

Control of herself, of her needs and desires, of her reactions. Kadir had a way of making a woman *want* to lose control. She was beginning to realize how very dangerous he was to her sense of well-being.

He frowned down at her. "There is no need to panic. I won't do anything to make you uncomfortable, Emily."

"Then why did you say—"

"I like teasing you," he said softly. "You are quite emotional, as it turns out. I had no idea."

Emily fought her natural inclination to drop her gaze from his. Instead, she pulled in a deep breath and kept her chin up. "I'm sorry, but this is outside my comfort zone. I know what to do when I'm your PA. I don't know what to do as your wife...especially your fake wife."

He put his hands on her shoulders and rubbed. Another jolt of sensation shot from where he touched her straight down to her sex. She wanted to whimper with it. Had she ever reacted this way to another man? Or was she just so deprived of contact lately that her body was starved for it?

"Just follow my lead and it will all work out."

She closed her eyes for a moment. She was in over her head. She should have realized it before. "I don't like deceiving your family. I should have said no."

"Ah, but you want the money."

She bit her lip. She wanted to explain herself, but he wasn't looking for an explanation. He was stating a fact. And mentioning her father's health issues would only distract attention from Kadir's problems right now.

"I do."

His hands dropped away from her shoulders and disappointment bit into her. He turned away and removed the flowing headdress. His dark hair was a sensual shock to her system, though she'd seen it a million times before. But there was something about the *kaffiyeh* and its removal that set up a drumbeat in her veins.

Kadir was thankfully oblivious as he set the fabric down and then continued into the outer suite where the seating area was. Once there, he collapsed onto one of the sofas and tilted his head back, his eyes closing. He looked troubled now, no longer angry or amused.

Emily's heart went out to him and she berated herself for being so insensitive. Of course he was troubled. His father was dying and she'd been going on about the sleeping arrangements like a timid virgin.

She walked over and perched on a chair nearby. She didn't know what to say, or if he'd even welcome her presence, but she had a need to be near him. His eyes opened again, a question in them.

"I didn't ask about your father," she blurted.

He shrugged, but she didn't miss the tension vibrating from him. "He is dying. He's frail, weak and shockingly wasted away from the man he was the last time I saw him."

"I'm sorry, Kadir."

"This is the way life is, *habibti*."

Yes, she certainly knew that. She thought of her father and the tense months while they'd waited for a donor heart. "Still, it cannot be easy for you."

His eyes glittered hotly. Angrily. "No, it isn't."

She licked her lips and ran her palms over her thighs. She was out of her depth here, trying to be friendly with the boss she'd only ever been professional with. Trying to be his wife and his companion and an understanding ear all at the same time.

All while worrying about her own problems. What was the matter with her? She did not need to burden Kadir with her own fears. He'd hired her for a job, she'd agreed, and she had no right to question the sanity of the arrangement now.

"If you want to talk—"

"I don't." His voice was firm, final.

Emily swallowed. She knew when he was dismissing her. She'd heard it a thousand times before, though it had never seemed so personal as it did right now. She got to her feet because it seemed the only thing she could do. "Well, then, I think I'll get ready for bed."

"Fine."

She started toward the bathroom, her ears burning

hot. How could she let him think she was such a selfish creature? How could she be so insensitive to his plight? She stopped and spun around again, her pulse beating a hot rhythm in her veins. "I'm sorry for complaining about the sleeping arrangements. I was just surprised by it."

He shrugged. "It is understandable. We did not discuss it prior to arriving."

He was too polite about it.

"But it's hardly something you should be thinking about right now. I should have been more sensitive."

His gaze was so intense she wanted to drop her eyes. She did not. "If you really want to give me something else to think about, invite me into the shower with you."

Emily swallowed hard. And then a thread of anger unwound inside her belly. She tried to be nice and he taunted her. Dismissed her apology as if it were nothing.

Which was his right, she decided. So she bit her tongue and gave him a regretful smile.

"I'm sorry, but I always shower alone. It's a rule of mine."

"Pity," he drawled.

Kadir went outside onto the balcony while Emily was in the shower and stood in the darkness for a long while. He'd gone to see his father, and he could still feel the shock of that moment when he'd beheld the once-strong king reduced to little more than a gaunt skeleton in an oversize bed.

His father had not smiled when he spoke, but then Kadir had not expected him to. King Zaid had never made it a secret that both his sons had become disappointments to him. Kadir less so than Rashid, but a disappointment nevertheless.

"I hear you have brought a woman with you," King Zaid had said, his voice stronger than Kadir would have thought possible.

"I brought my wife."

His father made a dismissive noise. "You have defied me, Kadir."

"I am in love, Father. I cannot live without her." A lie, but a necessary one.

"I see." King Zaid closed his eyes and swallowed. "I never thought you would disrespect my wishes as your brother has so often done. I thought you were the good son."

Kadir wanted to lash out, wanted to tell the old king that both his sons were good sons—but that he was too hard and proud and blind to realize it.

"A man will do things for love that he would not otherwise do." He should feel guilty for lying, but strangely he did not. "Besides, I've told you many times before that I often blamed Rashid for things I had done."

His father waved a weak hand as if annoyed. What Zaid did not want to hear, he did not hear. One of the reasons why his sons had left Kyr long ago.

"The succession is not decided," King Zaid rasped. "There is time for you to renounce this woman and take your place as king."

Kadir felt the chill of that pronouncement like a dip into an arctic pool. "I am not prepared to do so."

"And if I were to order it?"

"Choose Rashid, Father. He is the right man for the job."

His father spat—and then he began to cough. Kadir stepped forward, alarmed, but the nurse who sat nearby was there instead, offering King Zaid a glass of water and straightening his pillows.

"Leave me," his father said when he could speak again. Kadir had stalked out, furious with the stubbornness of his father and brother both. And perhaps even with himself. He should just go to the council and announce he was not going to accept the throne even if the king chose him, but he wanted very much for his father to make a different choice. A conscious choice.

Kadir wanted the king to pick Rashid, which would be the best choice for Kyr, and then he might feel as if he'd finally done something right by his brother. As if he'd righted the wrongs of their childhood in the palace. Perhaps the things he'd done were not so extreme when viewed through the lens of boyhood—but they felt like crimes against his own flesh. In seeking his father's approval, he'd actively encouraged the king's barely suppressed frustration with Rashid.

And Rashid had been too proud to fight back, which only exacerbated the situation.

After the meeting with his father, Kadir had returned to his room and found Emily fretting over the sleeping arrangements. She'd seemed so ordinary and normal that it had been everything he could do not to drag her into his arms and just hold her close. But she would not have understood, so he had not done it.

The night air whipped up from the sea, ruffling his hair, but it was not quite cool enough to dampen his heightened senses. He remembered their arrival on Kyrian soil. He could still feel Emily in his arms, still taste that kiss as they'd stood in the doorway to the plane. He wanted her with a sharpness that was uncharacteristic of him, and he didn't know why.

Kadir swore softly. He should not be thinking about this. How was he going to lie in a bed with her and not touch her? He was growing hard just thinking about it.

He told himself it was the stress of the current situation making him want her. Rewind the clock a day, and she would still be his PA, dressed in her stark suits and ugly shoes, and he would be none the wiser about what kind of woman lay beneath the professional polish.

He stood for a long time in the night air, until he was chilled and tired, and then he turned and went inside. The lights were dim and the room quiet. He shed the *dishdasha* he wore and padded over to the bed in his underwear. Emily lay on her side, as far from his side of the bed as possible. She was a small lump under the covers. Her hair, he was shocked to realize, was braided. He'd pictured it free, streaming over the sheets, but she'd very sensibly confined it.

Of course she had.

She had also lined the center of the bed with pillows. He didn't know whether to laugh or be offended. In the end, he flipped the sheets back and slid into the bed. And then he lay with his arms behind his head, staring up at the ceiling while his body continued to burn with inappropriate thoughts of her.

He did not know how long he'd lain there when she turned over.

"Are you okay?" Her voice was rough with sleep.

"Define *okay*."

"You've had a shock tonight. You must be feeling so many things."

"I am." Because what else could he say?

She sighed. "I know something about how it feels to get devastating news, and I know it can be hard to make sense of it."

"Do you?" He did not think she could possibly understand how he felt right now. Angry, frustrated, guilty, resigned.

"My father had a heart transplant five years ago. We weren't sure he would make it."

Kadir turned toward her. Out of everything he'd imagined her saying, this had not even made the top ten. How had she worked for him all this time and he'd never known this most important of things? She had never once mentioned it.

In fact, she never talked about anything personal. He realized, lying there in bed with her, a pile of pillows between them, that everything he knew about her was from observation and reading her personnel file. She was the person who was the closest to him on a day-to-day basis, who knew all his business secrets, and he didn't know her at all. It was a stunning realization.

"You never told me this before."

He could feel her shrug more than see it. "It was personal. And we don't exactly do personal chitchat, do we?"

"It would seem not. And yet I wish I had known."

"It's not a secret or anything, but it's not the kind of thing you just up and say either. There never was an appropriate moment to mention it before."

"And is he well now?"

"Well enough, yes. But I really wasn't trying to make this about me." She sighed. "I feel like I'm doing everything wrong. I just wanted you to know I understand how difficult this must be for you. I've done a poor job of that so far."

It was difficult, but not for the reasons she might imagine. Of course a part of him was upset that his father was dying. But their relationship had fractured so long ago that his father almost felt like a distant relative to him. He cared, but it wasn't going to devastate him when the inevitable happened.

No, the most difficult part for him now was in making sure he righted the wrongs he'd done to Rashid. Which his father seemed determined not to allow. He could walk away, certainly. But he wanted his father to choose Rashid because it was right.

How could he explain any of that to her? She'd asked him earlier if he wanted to talk. But what would he say? How could he begin to talk about such deeply personal things with anyone?

"You are close to your father?" he asked.

She hesitated for a moment, as if trying to figure out what he wanted from her. Or maybe she was just confused by the randomness of the question. "Yes."

Kadir let out a breath and rolled back until he was looking up at the ceiling again. There was something about lying in the dark with another person that made him want to confess his secrets. Not all of them, of course.

"I am not close to mine." It was a relief to say it, and yet he also felt as if he was admitting what a terrible son he was. She didn't say anything and he felt a coolness sweep over him. Followed by a needle of pain in his chest. This was why he did not engage in personal confessions with anyone. "You are shocked."

"No," she said in a rush. "Just sad for you."

Now he was the one who was shocked. He couldn't recall any of the women of his acquaintance feeling emotional *for* him. Over him, yes. But this was a novelty and he wasn't quite sure how to respond. "I have made my peace with this long ago. Not all relationships are perfect."

"No. In fact, I'd say none are. But some are better than others."

He wondered at the note of sadness in her voice. He

didn't think it was all for him. Still, he felt the need to lighten things up between them. Before he began spilling things he was not willing to share with anyone. Things that would reveal how damaged he truly was. "This is true. Take us, for example."

"Us?" She sounded surprised and he almost laughed.

"Yes, us. As my assistant, you are the perfect combination of competent and familiar."

She huffed. "But as your wife, I suck."

"I would not have put it quite that way. But no, you have not been very good at it thus far. Which I fail to understand. You are so good at being my assistant that I would have thought pretending to be my wife would come easy. Because you already know me."

"Maybe that's the problem," she grumbled. "I know you too well."

"And what does this mean?"

He heard the covers rustling and then she was sitting up, facing him. "Seriously?"

"Yes, seriously."

She made a noise that might have been disbelief. Or frustration. "I've witnessed far too many mornings after with you. I've escorted women to the door while you turn over and go back to sleep. And let's not forget Lenore and the scene with her—when was that? Just two days ago! It's hard to pretend to be the woman besotted with you when I know how that works out for so many of them. You humiliate them, Kadir. And then you forget them as soon as they're gone!"

Her words surprised him. No, he felt nothing for any of them. But he had not set out to hurt anyone. "You think I humiliate them?"

"Maybe you don't mean to," she said, her voice softer now. "But I think so."

He thought he should be offended, but mostly he was just weary. "And I think they know what they're getting with me. I make no secrets about what I want, Emily. I don't pretend to feelings I do not have."

"Then I think they don't hear that part. Or they hope they'll be the one to change your mind. Because they certainly seem shocked when it's over."

"And how is this my fault?"

She picked up one of the pillows and hugged it to her. "I don't know. I just feel badly for them. *Most* of them," she amended. He thought she might have punched the pillow. "Dammit, Kadir, I hate when you make sense. It's because I'm tired. Tomorrow, I'll think up the perfect answer to your question."

"Perhaps you will. But I doubt it. I'm not cruel, Emily. I never make promises. Any woman who gets involved with me knows that a long-term relationship is not on the menu."

He always made that clear, and yet he knew they didn't always believe it.

She lay down again and he heard her yawn. "I'm sure you're right. Poor things."

He wanted to keep talking, but he didn't know what else to say. Soon, her breathing deepened and he knew she was asleep. He was alone, as always, with his thoughts.

Or maybe he was just alone.

CHAPTER NINE

EMILY SLEPT LIKE the dead. And then she awoke as sun-light filtered through the shutters and crept across the bed to caress her face. She was warm and content. And for a moment at least, uncertain where she was. It wasn't unusual to wake up disoriented when work-ing for Prince Kadir al-Hassan. You could be in Paris today, Hong Kong tomorrow and Sydney the next day.

But she knew she wasn't in any of those places. And she knew something was different about this trip. It hit her simultaneously that two things were unusual. First, she was no longer Kadir's PA and she didn't have to leap out of bed and tend to his breakfast before waking him.

Second, there was a warm body pressing into hers and an arm slung over her waist. That was not at all correct. She hadn't been in the same bed with another human being in a very long time—unless she'd gotten drunk last night and picked up a stranger. She turned her head slowly, her heart beginning to pump harder. Because she knew the truth before her gaze landed on the face of the man whose body was curled around hers.

Kadir.

Emily's heart rocketed. She barely managed not to squeal. Her fingers wrapped around his hand and she started to lift it so she could slide out from under his

grip. But his eyes snapped open and she found herself
staring into his clear gray gaze.

He moved slightly and she felt the hard press of his
erection against her bottom. Emily gasped as blood
flooded her cheeks. It was followed by an answering
wetness in her feminine core that both shocked and
dismayed her.

"Salaam, habibti."

"You crossed the line," she accused. "You promised
you wouldn't."

One of his eyebrows arched. "Did I?" He lifted his
head to peek over her body. And then he lay on the pillow again. "I believe you need to look to your left."

Emily did so—and felt the burn of embarrassment
grow even hotter than it already was. The pillow line
was still there and she was facing it. Kadir had not
crossed her barrier; she had.

"I must have been cold," she sniffed. "You turned
the air-conditioning up so high."

"Because you told me to, if you will recall."

She tried to move away, but his arm tightened
slightly. "Kadir—"

"You have to admit it feels nice to wake beside someone. Comforting." He put his nose against her neck and
breathed.

Her pulse beat hard and fast. Emily closed her eyes
and swallowed. "That's beside the point."

"So you admit it feels nice?" His voice was a soft
rumble in her ear. And her body was snapping with
sparks that scared her.

"I didn't say that." Not precisely, anyway. She moved
against him, trying to pull away—and nearly groaned
as his erection pressed into her again. What would it be
like to just turn around in his arms and…?

No! She couldn't think like that. She could not, for one moment, allow that kind of breach in her personal code to happen. She tugged again...

And this time he let her go. She slipped across the sheets until she was back on her side of the pillows. Her heart thrummed as she sat up and tried to fake nonchalance.

"You do realize that's an effect of morning, yes?"

She turned to look down at him. He lay against the white sheets, his body dark and perfect. The covers were pushed down to his waist and his chest was gloriously bare. All those rock-hard muscles. And that damn arrow of hair dipping beneath his belly button.

She knew what lay down there and she experienced a pang of longing as she thought of him sliding the covers down the rest of the way, of her pressing her mouth to his abdomen and tugging off his briefs...

"What?" she asked after a long second in which she couldn't remember what he'd said.

"The erection. An effect of morning. And your shapely bottom wedged against me, I imagine."

Emily closed her eyes for a second and tried to get her racing heart under control. "You say the most outrageous things."

"Do I?" He wasn't smiling but she got the impression he was grinning at her anyway. "And here I thought I was being honest."

Emily pushed her braid back over her shoulder. "All right, you were being honest. And I'm sorry I crossed the pillows. I can only imagine I got cold. And I'm not used to sleeping with anyone else, so..."

She realized what she was saying—babbling, really—and ran out of words. Kadir's gaze gleamed.

"This is a shame, Emily. A woman as lovely as you shouldn't spend her nights alone."

"You are *such* a player."

He looked at her quizzically. "A player?"

His English was so good that she sometimes forgot he wasn't always conversant with all the idioms. "It means you're good at getting women to slip into bed with you. And that it happens often. Flattery is no doubt one of the tools in your arsenal."

"Ah. But you are already in bed with me. Why would I need to flatter you?"

"Don't be obtuse, Kadir. You know what I mean." Emily folded her arms over her chest, suddenly aware of her nipples pressing against the thin cotton of the tank top she'd worn to bed.

Kadir whipped the sheets back then and stood. Emily's mouth went utterly dry. He was tall, golden and perfectly formed. He was wearing the barest of black briefs—and they were stretched out in the front by an impressive erection. Oh, it was so unfair that he was so beautiful. And that she wanted him.

Emily licked her lips automatically and Kadir's gaze sharpened. She dropped her eyes and pretended to be unaffected. But her pulse was hammering so hard in her throat she was certain he must know.

Dammit. She'd been so careful—so *careful*—to keep Kadir compartmentalized in her head in the category of *boss: off-limits* that to suddenly realize he was no longer there was a shock. He'd moved into another compartment and she couldn't seem to move him back. This one was labeled *sexy male: need immediately.*

Emily closed her eyes and took a deep breath. Okay, this was a setback. But she could deal with it. She *would* deal with it. There was no other choice.

"I do know what you mean, Emily. But I like teasing you." She glanced at him and saw he'd tilted his head to watch her. "Your skin is the most interesting shade of pink right now."

Emily wanted to drag the covers over her head. "It's the sunlight coming into the room. And all this gold on the ceiling."

It was a lousy excuse, but hey, she wasn't going to admit she was thinking about him naked—about her wrapped around him naked—was she? Nooooo, not happening.

"Of course it is," Kadir said. He laughed softly as he went into the bathroom. Naturally, he did not close the door and she could hear the water falling against the tiles as he started the shower. She imagined Kadir sliding those briefs down his thighs and stepping under the spray.

Her sex throbbed with heat and need and she closed her eyes, forcing herself to take slow, deep breaths. It was only the second day of their sham marriage.

And already her purpose grew muddled and her will teetered on shaky ground.

Emily showered and dressed in the least sexy dress she could find in her wardrobe—which, she had to admit, didn't mean much. This dress had a square neck that didn't show any cleavage and a swirly skirt that flared out thanks to a tulle underskirt. But it was still form-fitting through the bosom and it hugged her curves like Kadir had this morning. Emily forced that thought from her mind as she stood in front of the mirror and surveyed the outfit.

The dress was chic and lovely, a vibrant turquoise, and she paired it with the lowest heels she could find in the closet. They were perhaps four inches high and nude. Not much lower, but somewhat easier to walk in than yesterday's snakeskin platforms.

"Not quite as sexy as I'd hoped, but still very unsuitable."

Emily spun to find Kadir in the door to the dressing room. He was dressed in traditional robes—a *dishdasha*—and the dark *kaffiyeh* of Kyr. Golden ropes—the *igal*—held the headdress in place. He looked every inch a sheikh, and so very unlike the boss she was accustomed to. There was something almost primitive about him now, though she chided herself for thinking so. Clothing did not change a man. This was his culture, not a costume donned for effect.

And yet it was having an effect on her.

She smoothed her fingers over the silk of her dress. "I like this dress."

"As do I. You look lovely, though you will certainly elicit disapproval from the old guard for being so vibrantly female."

Her heart skipped a beat. "You said *some* people would not approve of me. I hope you aren't setting me up for a huge breach of decorum so that every single person in Kyr will despise me."

He frowned. "I would do no such thing, Emily. You are still my wife. Your unsuitability rests primarily on your not being Kyrian. But yes, there will be those who are shocked by your clothing, your passion for me and your bright inner fire. They are the ones who will not approve." He came toward her then, and she realized he was holding a velvet box in his hand. "You are missing some things," he told her as he opened the box and set it on the table beside her.

Emily gasped at the sparkling diamonds nestled

against the black velvet. Her gaze lifted to Kadir's. "I can't wear those."

He frowned. "Of course you can. You will wear them." He took the diamond-and-platinum necklace and fitted it around her throat. She turned so he could clasp it, her heart beating wildly in her chest as his fingers skimmed the bare skin of her neck. The necklace fit close to her throat but it was only when she turned around that she realized it was a collar. And it glittered as though someone had turned on Christmas lights.

"This is too much, Kadir."

"Not for my wife it isn't." He ruthlessly went about clasping on a matching bracelet. And then he handed her a pair of diamond drop earrings that she fitted into her ears with shaking hands.

"Won't I look a bit gaudy for daytime?"

His eyes roved over her. "Not at all. You will look amazingly beautiful."

She glanced down at the bracelet—a sizable platinum-and-diamond concoction that caught the light and sparkled as crazily as the necklace—and realized what was missing. A wedding ring. Unless, maybe, they didn't wear them in Kyr?

As if he knew what she was thinking, Kadir produced another box from somewhere. A smaller box. This one he opened away from her. And then he set it aside and lifted her left hand. When he slid the giant diamond on her finger, she actually felt light-headed.

"This is insane. Someone will bash me over the head and take this stuff. And then you'll be right back where you started."

He laughed softly. "You are a princess of Kyr, Emily. No one is going to bash you over the head."

She shivered as she stared at the ring. It was lovely,

but a bit more ostentatious than she was accustomed to. The thought hit her that it was something her mother would have loved. And that was not a pleasant thought.

"I don't like this, Kadir. It feels...wrong somehow."

He took her by the shoulders and held her firmly. His eyes bored into hers. He was so very handsome, so commanding, and she felt herself melting beneath those eyes. "It's just a few days, *habibti*. You can do it. You may even have fun."

His head descended and she closed her eyes. When his mouth brushed over hers, she nearly swayed into him. Instead, she put her hand against his chest, though she wasn't sure whether it was to stop him—or to stop herself from leaning in closer.

The kiss was brief, an intense meeting of tongues that both shocked and aroused her, and then he pulled away and she found herself looking up into glittering eyes that had darkened several degrees. "For luck," he said.

Emily blinked. "We are alone," she answered almost breathlessly.

"I am aware of this."

"You kissed me. That's not part of the agreement."

He lifted an eyebrow imperiously and she realized that while he might not technically be her boss any longer, he was still a sheikh. And a prince. How many people argued with a prince?

His fingers ghosted over her cheek before dropping away. "You still don't quite understand. We are in Kyr, *habibti*. And you are my lawful wife. My property to do with as I wish."

Emily trembled deep inside. Because, for a moment, she wondered what it would be like for him to do whatever he wished. But she couldn't let him think she was growing soft. She drew herself up.

"I very much doubt an unsuitable wife is your property. If she were, she might be more suitable, yes?" Feeling a moment of inspiration, she lifted her hand and ran her fingers along his hard jaw. His eyes darkened and her breath caught in her lungs. "I own *you,* Kadir. This is why you brought me here. I own you, and your father will not approve."

He didn't say anything and her heart pounded while she waited for him to react. She couldn't tell what thoughts were crossing that brilliant mind of his. But then he laughed and relief washed through her.

"Touché, Emily." He took her hand and drew her to his side. "I believe you are ready now."

He led her out of the room and down a long hallway where servants scurried to and fro. He didn't walk too fast, for which she was thankful since he'd stripped her of her sensible shoes, and she found herself peering into ornate room after ornate room as they strode by.

The royal palace of Kyr was filled with priceless objects—marble and gold statues, intricately carved furniture, paintings, tapestries, and the most colorful rugs she'd ever seen. Some of them were huge and must have taken many years to weave. She knew enough about Oriental carpets to know they were not made on machines. Hundreds of women would have labored for many hours a day on the works of art gracing the palace floors.

Outside the soaring windows, the sky was a blazing, clear blue. The horizon shimmered with heat and the brown mountains in the distance appeared to wobble at their bases. Emily could see tall palm trees and a camel train plodding along. It was starkly different from any-where else she'd been with Kadir thus far.

But it had a compelling beauty of its own and she wondered at Kadir's seeming discomfort about re-turning to Kyr. Had his life in the palace been lonely? Harsh? Or maybe it was just boring and he much pre-ferred his life now.

She found herself suddenly wanting to know more about him, about who he'd been as a child and why he seemed so intent on presenting his father and the royal court with a bride of whom they would not approve. Because if she knew anything at all about him, it was that he was brilliant and capable. He would handle in-heriting a throne with the grace and skill with which he handled every business encounter she'd ever seen him in. Kadir was a born leader.

But Kadir wasn't going to give her a chance to ask any questions just now. Instead, he steered her into a giant room filled with milling people—who instantly stopped what they were doing and sank to their knees as a man in a uniform bellowed something. She would have gasped at the sight if not for Kadir giving her a warning look.

It was extraordinary to see so many people drop so quickly, to hear the rustling of their clothing and the hush that spread over the room. Emily's belly clenched tight as Kadir said something in Arabic. A second later, people rose, their gazes landing on her.

"Keep your chin up," Kadir murmured, tucking her arm into his and anchoring her to his side.

"What is this?" she whispered back as panic began to unwind inside her.

"The daily audience. My father cannot attend, of course, and he's asked me to do so in his stead."

"Audience? Does this mean you have to sit somewhere and receive them one by one?"

"No. This is a formality. Their petitions to the throne are filtered through the functionaries and addressed by the king and council in session. Rarely, one of them receives a private audience. This is merely for appearances."

Appearances. Emily gazed out over the crowd and felt her heart thrumming against her chest. Not because she wasn't accustomed to attending large gatherings with Kadir, though she was usually standing behind him with a notebook and pen, but because she was so visible. And garnering more than a few stares.

"I don't think they like me," she muttered.

Kadir smiled. Somehow, it seemed as if it was for her alone. She told herself it was just a part of the mirage.

"That is the plan, is it not?" He squeezed her hand. "Now come, let us mingle. And don't forget to hang on my every word."

"Except I won't understand a thing you say," she grumbled.

He dipped his head toward hers, his breath whispering against her ear. "Then you can gaze at me lovingly instead." His lips skimmed her cheek and sensation streaked down to her sex. It was shocking and alarming at once. If they weren't in public, she would...

Emily blinked. No, she wouldn't. She wouldn't do a damn thing.

She forced herself to smile up at him, aware they were the center of attention. "I'll do my best, Your Highness."

He stopped his forward motion and gazed down at her, his brows drawing together. "Your Highness? I thought we had an understanding."

She stood on tiptoe—odd to have to do that in heels, but there it was—and whispered in his ear. "Just reminding myself what's really happening here. You are the prince. I'm the hoochie mama."

He shook his head. "And here I thought I understood English. What is this hoochie thing, Emily?"

She could almost laugh at his confusion. Except the words hurt. She didn't know why she'd said them in the first place, or why it stung so much—no, that wasn't true. She did know. They made her think of her mother. Of what others had said about her mother when she'd run away with her lover.

Emily gave him a bright smile to hide her discomfort.

His eyes flashed hot. "You are not a hoochie mama. Or a whore, if I understand the meaning correctly."

She could feel tears pricking at the backs of her eyes. She should not be surprised he'd understood. "It was just a joke, Kadir."

His expression was fierce. "I won't allow you to make jokes like that. Not about yourself. Not when it upsets you."

She hadn't expected him to be so perceptive. Her impression of Kadir did not include sensitivity—or a desire to protect her. Once more, she had to revise her opinion of him. Her heart throbbed. "It's nothing. Forget I said it."

He tipped her chin up with a finger. Beyond him, she could see the people milling about almost impatiently. But Kadir didn't seem to care as he focused the power of his gaze upon her. He still looked fierce, and her heart swelled with feeling.

"You are my wife. A princess. You are beautiful and valuable. Don't forget it."

Emily throat was tight. "I won't."

But as Kadir led her into the crowd, his hand tight on hers, all she could think was that this was an act between them. A performance. That was what she couldn't forget. He did not mean to make her heart pound or her emotions roil with his intensity. He simply did it because that's what he always did to women. He conquered with words, with looks, with touches.

She could not allow herself to be conquered.

Emily decided to throw herself into her role as Kadir began to speak with different people. She would not fail him. She stayed by his side, smiling at people and chatting to those who spoke to her in English. Some people seemed uncertain what to think of her, but some of the women were openly curious and made no efforts to hide it.

Emily was relieved she was not the only woman in Western clothing or the only one wearing jewels. Some of the Kyrian women dressed in jeweled *abayas;* some covered their hair, and some did not. They were friendly and polite and she found herself interested in them and they in her. She did not sense that they disapproved of her or despised her. In fact, many of them seemed to enjoy talking with her.

Eventually, however, as the afternoon wore on, she and Kadir were surrounded by several older, serious-looking men who seemed content to pretend she did not exist. Emily frowned and tried not to concentrate on how much her feet were starting to hurt or how much she missed her low heels.

All she wanted was to sit down, but Kadir showed no signs of slowing. The men ignored her completely. After the warmth of the women, it made her feel unwelcome—and uncharitable. When she could take it no more, she put her hand in Kadir's to get his attention.

He stopped speaking instantly and turned to gaze down at her, a question in his eyes. If she were Lenore, she would have pouted and stuck out her lip, but Emily couldn't bring herself to behave that way. She was a good girl, not a self-centered drama queen.

Still, he expected her to be unsuitable. So she would do her best, especially as this small audience seemed tailor-made for such a performance.

"I'm bored, Kadir."

She could feel the men's gazes hardening and she knew they understood English perfectly well. Kadir's dark brows drew down. She wasn't sure if he was amused or irritated at her little outburst.

"And what would you prefer to do, my love?"

Emily's heart throbbed as she stepped closer to him and trailed a finger up his arm. "I think you know, darling."

This time an eyebrow arched. "Do I? Perhaps you should tell me what you want."

She stood on tiptoe and put her lips against his cheek. It was naughty and exhilarating and she liked it far too much. "I suppose I should say I want you desperately, but those awful men can't hear me now so I'll just say that my feet hurt and I'm tired of feeling shut out of this conversation."

He caught her around the waist and dipped his head to her ear. A shiver ran down her spine when his breath caressed the shell of her ear. "I wish you really did want me desperately. Because I'd love to strip you, Emily. Strip you and lick you from head to toe."

She almost backed away from him. Except that would give away the game and she couldn't do it. Not only that, but she didn't *want* to do it. She liked the way it felt to have him so close. Her sex flooded with wetness as a thrill shot through her, filling her with heat.

"You're a bad man, Kadir."

His voice came out as a growl. "You have no idea, Emily. No idea."

"Oh, I think I do. Just not from inside information, so to speak."

He nipped her ear and she gasped. Her body throbbed.

"The moment you want that *inside* information, I'm yours. Now go, before I do something the likes of which will scandalize Kyr for the next fifty years."

Emily backed away slowly as his hands slid from her body. She stood there for a long moment looking at him, and he at her, her body aching in ways she'd forgotten. His eyes blazed and part of her, the part that sparked and burned, suddenly wanted to catch his hand and lead him away with her.

"Emily?"

His voice was filled with promise—and with just enough of a question to break the spell. What was she doing standing here and staring at him as though he was the last glass of water in the desert?

Emily turned and fled. When she reached their room, she went into the bathroom to lean over the sink and splash her face with cold water. If she didn't cool this fire raging inside her, there was no telling what she might do when Kadir turned up again.

CHAPTER TEN

KADIR THREW THE phone down in disgust. He'd called Rashid again, and again Rashid had not answered. It was five days since they'd arrived in Kyr, and there was no sign of his brother. What was Rashid doing? Had he changed his mind about coming? Was he just going to let the throne go without a fight, or was he making a statement by taking his time?

If Rashid did not arrive soon, it would be too late. Their father was growing weaker by the hour. And more insistent that Kadir divorce Emily and take the throne. Kadir was furious and frustrated. But he had to acknowledge that perhaps he was well and truly trapped. If Rashid no longer wanted to be king, if he'd decided he was finished with their father, with Kyr and even with Kadir himself, there was nothing Kadir could do but accept the responsibility.

His deception had only been meant to steer his father toward Rashid as the logical choice, but if Rashid did not come, there was no choice. Kyr could not go ungoverned by an al-Hassan. They had been this nation's leaders for centuries. And Kadir would not allow it to change, though his life would transform so drastically. To walk away now would plunge Kyr into chaos because there was no one else who could lead. No one but the council, and it would fracture as each member tried to put forth his own candidate for the throne.

No, Kadir would not allow that, though it would mean the end of everything he'd worked for. And the end of his time with Emily.

Emily. Just thinking of her made him as restless as a caged leopard.

Quite simply, Kadir was going mad with desire for his fake wife. He'd spent the last few days getting hard at the sight of her. And many nights going to bed frustrated. After that first night, he'd stuck to his side of the pillow wall and she to hers, but it was sheer torture. He lay there willing her to come across the barrier since he'd sworn he wouldn't do so, but she never did.

His days were so busy now that he hardly saw her, except at functions they attended together. He was beginning to regret the impulse to dress her in beautiful, fitted clothing. It not only made him physically uncomfortable, but it also made him angry as hell when he caught some other man staring at her.

Her clothes were fashionable, not at all trashy or— what had she said?—something a hoochie mama would wear. It shamed him that she had thought he wanted such a thing for even a moment.

The clothing Guido chose for her showcased her figure in ways that had Kadir imagining his hands on her. On the high swells of her breasts, the delicate curve of her waist, the arch of her hips. Hell, even her bare calves, accentuated by the high heels he'd insisted she wear, inflamed him.

What had he been thinking? He shoved a hand through his hair in frustration. Clearly, he had not. Or he'd thought he was made of sterner stuff where she was concerned. Idiot.

Though it had been only a few minutes since he'd tried to call Rashid, Kadir snatched up his phone and checked his messages, the same as he'd been doing all day.

Of course there was nothing. If Rashid wanted to punish him, he'd picked the perfect way to do it.

"Kadir?"

He turned at the sound of Emily's voice. She stood in the door to the private courtyard off their suite of rooms, where he had retreated to call Rashid. His blood beat at the sight of her. She was wearing a body-hugging black dress, her breasts wedged firm and high in the bodice, her dark hair loose, his diamonds sparkling at her throat and ears. He glanced at her hand, felt a current of possessiveness wash through him at the sight of his ring on her finger.

It wasn't real, he reminded himself. And yet it was the most real thing in his life right now. *Emily* was the most real thing in his life.

He tamped down on his wayward desire and leveled her with an even look so she would not sense his turmoil. "Yes, *habibti?*"

She twisted her fingers together in front of her. He was learning that Emily contained depths of emotion he'd never suspected. And part of how she kept it in check was with her nervous fidgeting.

"I was just wondering how you are."

He sat and leaned his head back against the soft cushions of the couch that perched on one side of the courtyard. "Well enough. You?"

She came over and stood nearby, though she did not sit. "I'm all right. The tea with the governing council wives was somewhat awkward."

He felt as if he should apologize. But what would be

the point? They both knew why she was here. If only Rashid would come, the plan would work perfectly. "I am certain you managed it with aplomb."

She blew out a breath. "It wasn't that bad, truly. A couple of them don't seem to care for me, but the others...well, some of them are quite nice. They seem to understand how strange this must be for me as an outsider."

He looked up and met her soft green gaze. He had asked a lot of her in coming here. And he'd not prepared her nearly well enough. "You must despise me."

"No, of course not."

He sat forward, his eyes searching hers. "It's all right. You can admit it."

She sighed. "I don't despise you, Kadir. I actually like some of the people I've met. It hasn't been nearly as bad as I thought it would be. But I hate deceiving them. I'll be glad when it's over." As if she realized what she'd just said, her mouth snapped closed. "I'm sorry, I didn't mean that. For this to be over, your father—"

He stood and put a finger over her lips, silencing her. Her mouth was soft but he resisted the urge to slide his finger along her lips. Somehow, he resisted. "I understand what you mean. And I share the sentiment."

Her eyes were troubled. "I shouldn't have said it."

He tilted his head back and gazed up at the slice of blue sky visible above the walls and minarets. There was no point in hiding the truth from her. "I am going to be king. It's inevitable."

Because Rashid wasn't coming, their father was slipping in and out of consciousness with more regularity, and the council was growing restless with the uncertainty of the situation. Kadir had to act before the council splintered under the strain.

He heard her pull in a breath. "Oh, Kadir. I tried to be unsuitable, I really did. But sometimes I've just been me, and that clearly hasn't been enough."

Her head was bowed, her hands clenched into fists. He tipped her chin up and forced her to look at him. "You have not failed, Emily. You've done a brilliant job." He ground his teeth in frustration. "It is I who have failed. And it's time to accept my fate and get on with it."

She was looking at him with an admiration he didn't expect. "You'll be an excellent king."

He wanted to laugh. "You have no reason to think so. You are being kind."

Her eyes widened indignantly. "Of course I do! I've never seen anyone talk so many people into doing things his way as you have over the last four years. If that's not a skill a king needs, then I don't know what is. You'll be great at it, because you are great at everything else."

"I am apparently not great at some things." When she frowned at him, he wanted to kiss her. But he did not, because he wasn't certain he could stop at just a kiss. "I am not great at everything, Emily, because you continue to sleep on your side of the bed. If I had my way, you would sleep wrapped around me."

A blush spread across her cheeks. "You already know you're irresistible to women. You don't need me to prove it yet again."

"But I am not irresistible to you."

"You're not my type. Tall, handsome, kingly." She shook her head. "Oh, no, I like my men short and quiet and willing to be bossed around."

"Emily," he growled, the idea of her having a type—especially a type that wasn't him—burning a hole in his gut.

"Stop worrying, Kadir. You're handsome and re-markable and fabulous. And you'll be the best king that Kyr has ever had. I just know it."

She was being prickly with him, but her praise warmed him deep inside. He didn't feel as though he was the best at anything right now. Oh, he could build skyscrapers that no one else could, but that wasn't running a kingdom.

If his skill at personal relationships was any indication, he was doomed to failure. He had a contentious relationship with his father, an apparently nonexistent one with his brother—and then there was Emily. She was the person who'd worked the closest to him for the longest time. Until just a few days ago, he would have said she did not like him much.

And now? Now she felt sorry for him. He could hardly bear it.

"Sit with me," he said, catching her hand and pulling her down with him. It wasn't a big settee and she ended up right beside him, her hip crowding against his. Her eyes were wide as she blinked at him.

He held his arm out, daring her to come into the circle of his embrace. He desperately wanted to be close to someone right now. Close to her. He expected her to trot out their agreement, to shoot up off the settee and stammer about an appointment or something. But she didn't. She folded herself against him as if she always did so, as if it were as natural as breathing, and he closed his eyes on a rough sigh.

"Thank you," he said against her hair, and she wrapped one arm tentatively around his waist. A simple touch, and yet he burned deep inside for more. "When my father dies, you will need to remain for the funeral. After that, I will divorce you and you'll be free to go."

Just saying the words sent a chill washing over him.
He wasn't certain if Emily trembled or if it was simply
the strength of his emotions making him think so. She'd
been a part of his life for long enough that he couldn't
quite imagine it without her. But he was resigned to
his fate and he had to let her know what came next for
her. For them.

He would miss her, but in time it would ease.

"Whatever you think best," she said, her voice muf-
fled against his robes.

"I'll wire the money into your account. And I'll give
you references."

Even as he said it, he knew he would give her enough
money so she wouldn't have to work again if she did not
want to. She could take her father to Florida and live
there with him if she chose. It hadn't been a part of the
plan, but he couldn't bear to send her back to Chicago
with only what they'd agreed upon. He didn't want her
to work for anyone else. He wanted her to do whatever
she wanted in life.

"Thank you," she said. He thought she sniffed. A
moment later, she was pushing herself away from him.
Her eyes were watery, though she did not let a single
tear fall. "I think I have a headache. I should go inside
and rest."

He wanted to reach out and trace her cheek with his
finger. And then he wanted to do so much more. He
kept his hands to himself. "Yes, perhaps you should."

She stood and smoothed the dress over her body
and he found himself aching to span her hips with his
hands, to press his mouth right against her belly. To
drag it lower until she screamed his name with passion
rather than frustration.

But he would do none of these things.

"I'm sorry, Kadir."

He looked up into her soft green eyes and had the strangest sensation when he imagined those eyes gone from his life. It was as if a piece of his soul had withered and died.

"So am I, *habibti*."

Two days later, the king of Kyr died in the middle of the night. His passing was peaceful and quiet, but the aftermath was not. Emily was shaken awake during the dark hours. She was disoriented, groggy, and her eyes felt gritty with the silent tears she'd spilled into her pillow.

"We must leave, Emily," a deep voice said, and a current of alarm prickled inside her as she recognized the urgency in Kadir's tone.

"What's wrong?"

"My father has passed."

She sat up immediately as the last veil of sleep fell away. "Oh, Kadir, I am so sorry."

He stood there, tall and remote, already dressed in his desert robes, and she wondered if he'd even been to bed. The last she recalled, he'd been working on his computer when she'd gone to bed earlier. He'd had trouble sleeping lately and he often stayed up late to work.

She thought that he also spent time trying to track down his brother, hoping that he would get a last-minute reprieve. But now it was too late. Rashid had not come and their father was dead. Kadir was truly the next king of Kyr.

"It's fine," he said coolly. "I'm fine. But we have to journey to the King's Oasis. It is required that I spend the next twenty-four hours there, isolated from the court. You are the only one permitted to go with me."

"Of course," she said, throwing back the covers and

hurrying to get dressed. She didn't think it mattered much now, so she donned jeans and tennis shoes. She grabbed a jacket and put it on over her T-shirt because it was cold in the desert at night.

Within half an hour, they were packed and in a Land Rover. When Kadir said they were going alone, he meant it. There were no servants with them, no caravan of vehicles as they began the journey into the dark desert.

She didn't know what to say, so Emily leaned her head against the window and gazed up at the stars. They were so plentiful out here, away from the city lights. A shooting star blazed across her field of vision and she made a quick wish.

She wished that Kadir would not send her away. A stupid wish, but there it was. She'd realized over the last several days that she cared about him. She couldn't imagine her life without him in it. And yet she had to do just that, because he would be a king and she was not needed. Or wanted.

She gritted her teeth against the fantasy that he might decide to keep her with him. *Oh, for goodness' sake, you're just as bad as all those other women, wanting what he cannot give.*

Not only that, but she knew she would not be welcomed in Kyr as a permanent part of his life—and certainly not as his queen. While there were people who seemed to like her, even welcome her, the governing council did not. They'd frowned at her and ignored her and clearly did not approve of her. Which was precisely as Kadir had wanted it.

Truly, if she'd been swathed head to toe in black robes, she still didn't think they would have liked her. She was too foreign in their eyes, and certainly not good enough for a prince of Kyr. That was the true measure of her unsuitability, not her clothing or her actions or anything else she did or did not do.

Emily closed her eyes and somehow managed to fall asleep against the bouncing of the vehicle. When Kadir awoke her later, the first rays of dawn were beginning to peek over the horizon. They drove into the oasis and she was surprised to find it wasn't empty, as she'd thought it might be, but filled with tents and animals. A couple of dark bodies moved between the animals, feeding them.

Kadir exited the Land Rover and stood beside it. Emily climbed out, her feet landing with a squish in the sand. She walked around to Kadir's side and stood there as a tall, dignified man in dark robes made his way to them. He was worn and weathered, his face brown and wrinkled with sun and wind. His eyes, however, were dark and glittering as he looked at them both.

Kadir spoke to the man, and his old eyes drifted closed. Then he sank to his knees and intoned something in Arabic. Kadir reached out and touched his shoulder and the man stood again. Soon, other men appeared and the contents of the Land Rover were whisked into a tent set aside from the rest.

Kadir turned to her and held out his hand. Emily slipped her hand into his and let him lead her inside the tent. It was opulent, with colorful carpets blanketing the floor and walls. Copper and gold gleamed on tables and in low cabinets. There were cushions spread liberally across the floor for seating, and a separate area that contained a large bed covered in furs.

The oil lamps were lit and the soft scent of incense wafted to her nose. Someone brought a tray with food and coffee and then disappeared. The man who had greeted them was the last to go and Emily found herself blinking at Kadir and wondering what would happen now. Twenty-four hours in the oasis. For what?

She wanted to go to him, wrap her arms around him and hold him tight, but she didn't dare. Because she didn't know if she could stop once she did.

"How are you feeling?" she asked softly.

Kadir spun toward her, his eyes sparking with emotion. "How am I feeling? Trapped."

It wasn't quite what she'd expected. "I don't know what to say to you, other than I'm sorry."

Kadir closed his eyes and tilted his head back. And then he said something she didn't understand. When he shook his fist at the top of the tent, she assumed it was probably something she didn't want to hear anyway. He was angry and emotional and she understood that he needed to vent.

"Do you want to know what the worst part is?" he said suddenly, his gaze hard on hers again. Daring her, maybe.

"What?"

"I think I got what I deserved."

Emily's heart squeezed at the raw pain in his voice. "I'm not sure I understand you."

He shook his head. She didn't think he would speak, but then suddenly the words tumbled from him. "I am a rotten brother, Emily. And when I tried to make it right again, Rashid did not come. I tried to make sure the throne was his, as it should be, but it no longer matters. My father is dead, Rashid is not here and the council will formally choose me before the world—if my father did not leave a will already proclaiming me heir. He claimed he had not chosen, but I believe he did. I think the old bastard was just manipulating us one last time."

Emily tried not to be shocked, but she knew she hadn't succeeded when one corner of his mouth curled in a hard smile.

"I failed to tell you what kind of dysfunctional family I have, didn't I? Well, here it is—my father is dead, and I don't feel much of anything at the moment but anger. And not for the reasons you would suppose." He clenched his hands into fists as his side. "He wasn't a kind man, or a loving man. He was exacting and proud, and though I loved him when I was a child, I grew to fear him. And then I despised him."

She couldn't imagine feeling that way about her father, but her mother was a different story. She'd been angry with her mother for years now.

"If you mean to shock me, you are doing so. But not for the reasons you suppose."

"You aren't horrified to your sweet little core that I couldn't stand the man who left me a crown? That his death doesn't bother me nearly as much as the situation I now find myself in?"

"I didn't live your life, Kadir. It's not my place to decide how you should be feeling right now."

He laughed. It was a bitter, angry sound. And then he ripped his headdress off and tossed it on the cushions. "Damn, Emily, I wish we'd been more honest with each other a long time ago."

Her heart beat hard. "That's not the kind of relationship we had."

He stalked toward her, stopped before he got too close. He vibrated with suppressed energy. "No, it's not. But I wish it had been." His gaze slid down her body, back up again. "I wish I'd noticed what was under those dull suits of yours. I wish I'd taken your hair down years ago and plundered your mouth until you begged me to strip you naked and kiss the rest of you."

Emily's breath shortened. "You don't mean that. You're just angry and upset—"

He moved closer and her voice died in her throat. All he had to do was reach out and touch her. She found herself wishing he would do so. Holding her breath waiting for him to do so.

And wondering how to say no if he did.

"I am angry, but I've wanted you for days now." He picked up the braid she always wore to bed and undid the elastic while her heart pounded hard. Then he started to unbraid her hair, shaking it loose with his fingers until it flowed over her shoulders and down her back. "I think I've wanted you for a very long time."

Emily swallowed. "Don't say that. You didn't look at me twice before Guido—"

"I did look, Emily. I looked a lot. And yes, I brought Lenore home—so many women home—but I looked at you and I wondered what it was about you. Why I was comfortable with you. Why I tried to provoke a reaction out of you. Why it made me happy when you frowned at anyone I was with. Why I looked forward to mornings and you being there—"

Emily cried out as she put a hand over his mouth. She couldn't bear to think of any of it just now. To think of it ending. "Stop! Don't say these things. Don't make me want…"

He took her arm and tugged her closer. His mouth landed on the inside of her wrist, his breath against her skin. A fiery current of need shot down her spine and into her sex as his tongue slid over her.

"Want what, Emily? This?"

He licked her skin again and an answering shudder

rolled through her. She had never, not once in her whole life, wanted a man as desperately as she wanted this one. It was crazy but true. She'd had boyfriends, she'd had sex—though not in a very long time—and she knew what it felt like to be wanted and to want.

But oh, God, not like *this*. Not as if every nerve ending she possessed was on fire. Not as if she needed this man to breathe, to survive. Not as if she would never be happy if she didn't have him.

And yet how could she do this with him and survive it? Because they were finished and she had to walk away soon. No, he would *send* her away soon. He had to. They'd failed and she had to go so he could be king.

"We can't." The words were wrenched from her.

He dragged her into his arms then, dragged her hips against his body until she felt the strength of his need for her. His voice was thick. "Why not? Why not just this once?"

Emily put her forehead against his chest, felt the quick beat of his heart. There was nothing she could say except the truth. "Because I'm afraid it will destroy me."

He pushed her back and searched her gaze. She was too weary to care what he saw there. Did she love him? Maybe she did. She didn't really know anymore what this feeling was or why it made her so desperate. She'd thought she was afraid of herself, afraid of what she might become if she let her hair down and allowed the sensual creature inside her to emerge from the shell again—but maybe she was afraid of him, of what he could do to her.

To her heart. Oh, she was no match for a man like Kadir. She'd worn her defenses around her like a shield for so long and she'd grown weary. Living with him these last few days had destroyed any pretense she had of not liking him.

He pushed her hair back off her cheeks and cupped her jaw in both his hands. The look he gave her was filled with so many emotions: tenderness, frustration, rage, desire. Finally, he took a deep, shuddering breath before tilting her head down to kiss her on the forehead.

Then he backed away from her and grabbed the head-dress he'd tossed aside before striding from the tent.

CHAPTER ELEVEN

THE SUN SANK below the horizon again before Kadir returned. Emily shot up from the cushions, her heart in her throat. He'd been gone all day and she'd been worried about him. But no one at the oasis understood her queries for his whereabouts. They brought her tea and food, and left her alone for long hours.

"Kadir." She somehow managed to say his name even as tears filled the back of her throat. "I was worried about you."

He looked weary as he waved a hand dismissively. "It is part of the ritual, *habibti*. I have been in prayer from sunup to sundown."

She let out a shaky breath. "I did not know. I thought…" She shook her head. "Never mind. Are you hungry? One of the women has just brought food."

"Yes, most definitely."

"Sit, then. I'll get it for you."

He took a seat on the cushions and she brought the tray with meat and cheese and fruit over to the low table in the center. Then she poured cool water into glasses and handed him one.

He took a long drink and set the glass on the table. She refilled it.

"I apologize for not explaining the ritual to you," he said.

She shrugged and studied the food. What could she say to him? That she'd missed him? That she'd been worried about him? That she'd spent the last several hours filled with regret that she'd pushed him away? "It's fine. I'm just glad you're well."

He reached out and touched her hand and her nerve endings tingled in response, flooding her senses with too much heat, too much emotion. She was such a mess, and all because of him.

"I left rather abruptly. I'm sorry."

"I don't know that I gave you any choice."

"I would never want to cause you pain, Emily."

"I appreciate that."

But she hadn't been able to stop thinking about the things he'd said to her earlier. He'd said he wanted her, that he'd been thinking about her for far longer than she realized. She wanted it to be true, and yet she doubted. But did it honestly matter? Once this was over, once they went back to the palace and he took his place as king, it was the end. She would leave Kyr and probably never see him again.

And that thought nearly doubled her over as fresh pain streaked through her body, curling and writhing in her belly, her limbs. It had been this way each time the thought crossed her mind today. Never see Kadir again? Never hear his voice stroke across the syllables of her name?

It was unbearable. Except that she had to learn to bear it. Somehow.

Emily picked up a handful of grapes. When she plucked one and held it up to Kadir's mouth, she thought she might melt at the heat flaring in his eyes.

"Emily," he said softly. "What is this?"

She looked at her hand. "I believe it's a grape. But don't quote me on that."

He snorted softly. But then he leaned forward and took the grape from her fingers with his mouth, his eyes never leaving hers. She plucked another grape and fed it to him, and then another, her heart skipping wildly in her chest.

The next time she fed him, he gripped her hand and sucked her index finger. Emily gasped as her body became a lightning rod. Sweet sensation streaked from her finger down to her sex and her feminine core grew wet as his tongue swirled and licked.

It was perhaps the most innocuously erotic thing anyone had ever done to her.

"You play with fire, *habibti,*" Kadir murmured when he finally let her go. "My control is not so strong right now."

Her heart raced a little bit faster than before. She could admit the truth, or she could push him away again. "I'm not sure mine is either."

Insane to divulge such a thing. Dangerous. But if she left this oasis without ever knowing what it was like to be Kadir's lover, just for one night, she would never forgive herself.

His eyes glittered in his devastatingly handsome face. "What has changed your mind?"

She dropped her gaze, her pulse throbbing hard. "Regret. I don't want any."

He put a finger under her chin and brought her head up to meet his gaze. "And what if you regret giving yourself to me?"

"I'll find that out in the morning, won't I?" She put her hand on his chest, smoothed his robes against the hard muscles beneath. "Besides, I rather thought we could give ourselves to each other. I didn't exactly intend to be passive."

With a growl, he pushed her back on the cushions until her body was beneath his, until the delicious weight of him pressed her down and made her shiver because she knew what was coming next. He spanned her rib cage with his broad hands. "Emily, I ache for you."

How thrilling it was to hear those words from his mouth. *For her.* "And I for you," she said breathlessly.

His mouth claimed hers in a hot, wet, deep kiss that made her back arch up off the cushions. "There's nothing here I want more than you," he said urgently, kissing her again and again while she moaned and writhed beneath him.

There was nothing—*nothing!*—better than having the full power of Kadir al-Hassan focused on her. Oh, no wonder all those women had lost their minds....

No, she told herself. *You will not think of that, of them. You will think of nothing but him.*

And it wasn't difficult, not really. Not when his mouth performed such magic on her. He kissed her like a man starved, demanding her passion, her soul. Their tongues met, dueled again and again, sucked each other deep and hard. He found the hem of her shirt and tugged it up and over her head. She thought he would move to her breasts, but he kept kissing her while she wriggled beneath him, flexed her hips and found his hardness. His groan was gratifying.

Emily tried to get her hands beneath his robes, but they were too voluminous and she made a choked sound of frustration. Kadir rocked back on his heels and ripped everything over his head until all that was left was a pair of briefs with a mouthwatering bulge....

Oh my...

"There is nothing in this world more exciting than to have a woman look at me as you are doing right this moment."

Emily's gaze flew to his and she realized she'd been staring. Drooling, perhaps.

"You're a beautiful man, Kadir. Any woman would look at you like I am right now."

"Yes, but I find it's more satisfying when it's you."

He crawled over her again, lowered all that glorious flesh down onto hers, and she gasped when his naked torso met her skin. She was still wearing her bra and jeans, but right now she wanted to be free of everything and just feel her naked body against his. She ran her hands up his sides, her heart throbbing at the fact she was finally caressing his skin, his muscles.

Kadir was beautifully formed, and he knew it. Right now, she didn't care that he knew. She only cared that she was finally, finally getting to touch him the way she'd dreamed.

A part of her hated that anyone else had touched him like this. She focused on her hands, on the way her skin was so light against his darkness. He caught one of them and brought it to his lips.

"You are thinking too much, Emily. About other women, other nights. This is about us. There is only you and me here tonight. And there is no one else I'd rather be with."

She ran her fingers over his sensual lips. "I've spent four years escorting women out of your bedroom. You can't expect me to forget that. Or to forget that I'm no different than they are after all. Wanting you. Craving you. Going mad with the thought of having you."

His smile was tender. "You are *very* different." He

dipped his lips to her throat and she arched her neck, moaning softly. "Because I am mad with the thought of having *you*. And that, you may rest assured, is not a common occurrence."

He flexed his hips against her center and she caught her breath at the feelings rolling through her. He made her feel special, though she told herself it was only a line. He was good at this, so good.

"The things I want to do to you, Emily," he said on a groan. "This night is not nearly long enough."

He kissed her again, his mouth taking hers in a hard, deep kiss. Emily arched up to him, wrapped her arms around him until he slipped her bonds and pressed openmouthed kisses to her neck, her collarbone, the valley between her breasts. Her bra had a front clasp and he did away with it handily. A moment later, his hot mouth was on her aching nipple. Emily cried out as she arched her back, thrusting herself greedily into his mouth.

He sucked hard and soft, nibbled and bit until her body was on fire. How could so much pleasure come from such a tiny spot? But he didn't stop there. He did the same to her other nipple until she was writhing on the cushions and panting his name.

When he unzipped her jeans and tugged them down her hips, she had a crazy moment of panic that she was completely naked before him. He knelt and peeled her jeans and panties off and dropped them. His gaze flicked over her and her breath caught in her throat while she waited for him to say something.

"Emily." He caressed her calves, her knees, the insides of her thighs as he moved over her body again. "So lovely. How stupid I have been not to make love to you before now."

"It wouldn't have happened." She sounded breathless. "Not while I worked for you. And if it had, I would have handed in my resignation."

He blinked. But he didn't stop caressing her. "Then perhaps it's good we have waited." He pushed her knees apart, his gaze dropping to the juncture of her thighs. "But we have much to make up for."

He bent and pressed a kiss to the inside of her thigh. Emily's body felt tight, like a rubber band stretched just under the breaking point. Another inch, and she would snap. Her breath came in tight, shallow little gasps and her skin burned with excitement.

Kadir's breath against her thigh was hot and moist— and then his fingers found her, his thumb skimming over her clitoris while she gasped.

"You like that," he murmured.

"Oh. Oh, yes."

He did it once more, and again her body tightened. "And what will you do if I lick you, Emily? Will you come for me?"

She was so aroused it physically hurt. Her body throbbed with pain and need and all she wanted was for him to ease the ache. She nodded, unable to speak.

His grin was wicked—and beautiful. He pushed her thighs farther apart. And then he bent and licked the wet seam of her sex.

Emily's back arched off the cushions as if someone had touched her with a live wire. The sound coming from her throat was high-pitched and desperate.

And she didn't care. She wanted more. She wanted everything.

Kadir tongued her again and again, until she was fisting giant handfuls of cushion and panting his name. She was so, so close, her body wound tighter than any spring ever could be—but Kadir was skilled and he knew how to keep her from soaring over the edge.

"Kadir," she begged. "Please."

He stopped abruptly, getting to his feet while she cried out. She lay there in shock while he walked out of the room. But then he was back, ripping open a condom and shoving his briefs down before rolling it onto his thick length.

Emily's heart beat harder as he stretched out over top of her again, pressing her into the cushions. His hand went between their bodies, stroked the bud of her sex.

"I have to be inside you, Emily. The first time you come with me, I want to feel it happening."

He captured her mouth, his tongue sliding deep. He tasted like her and it made her feel wildly possessive. She kissed him harder and he responded with a surge of passion that left her breathless.

A moment later, she felt the head of his cock and she reached between them, both to touch him and to guide him into her. He stiffened as she wrapped her hand around him, and then he groaned when she pumped her fist over him once, twice.

In response, he hooked an arm behind her knee and spread her wide before plunging into her. Emily tore her mouth from his as a scream erupted from her throat. Her body was so ready for him, so primed and on edge, that she came immediately, shuddering around him while he rocked into her in short, quick strokes that dragged out her release.

"That's it," he said thickly. "Like that. Lose yourself in it, Emily."

It had been so long since she'd had an orgasm that it seemed to last and last and last. But it ended finally and she went limp beneath him. He kissed her cheeks, her nose, her jaw.

"You needed that."

She managed a laugh. "Yes."

He was still deep inside her, his body as hard as stone. "Has it been a long time?"

She moved her hips, surprised when fresh fire streaked through her. "There was no time for dating while working for you."

He spanned her hip with a broad hand and shifted her upward before stroking into her again. She moaned with pleasure.

"I am very glad for this," he said tightly. "I cannot imagine you with anyone but me."

He moved hard inside her then, branding her with the strength of his possession. Emily wrapped her legs high around his back, locking her ankles as he drove into her harder and faster, building the tension all over again. She didn't think her body could respond so quickly to this fresh assault on her senses, but once again she was surprised by how well Kadir seemed to know her.

Their bodies strained together, rising and falling and melting, over and over, until Emily couldn't hold on another moment. She spun out of control with a cry, falling off the edge and into the blackness below. She thought she might have sobbed his name, but she couldn't be sure. Her every sense was suddenly overwhelmed with pleasure—and love so sharp it sliced her to ribbons inside.

"Emily," he said in her ear, his voice urgent and tight. And then it broke as he found his own release, his body shuddering deep inside hers. He said her name again, but it cleaved in half with a groan.

She lay beneath him, stunned with the intensity of

everything she was feeling. She was wrapped in his heat and the scent of sex, her body shuddering, her pulse pounding. All her worst fears had come true, in spite of her caution.

Kadir took everything from her, turned her inside out and shone a light on all the dark corners she'd tried to keep hidden. But she couldn't deny the truth of her feelings anymore.

She'd tried so hard not to fall in love with him. She'd convinced herself for years that she despised him, that he was a playboy with no feelings and no heart and that he was beneath her contempt.

But it wasn't true. He had feelings and he was as lost and alone as anyone, no matter how hard he tried to hide it from the world. If not for that, she could have remained apart. She could have kept her heart intact. But she'd fallen in love with Kadir al-Hassan, and she never wanted to be anywhere but here, lost in this tent in the desert with him.

Sadness overwhelmed her then. She would never have a life with him beyond tonight. There was no future with Kadir. Even if he was not going to be the king of Kyr, there was no future with him.

Because this was what he did—he broke women on the rocks of his passion, made them feel special and wonderful, and then he cut them loose without a backward glance.

Emily closed her eyes and swore she would not cry. She could spin up a fantasy where she spent the next several weeks in Kadir's bed, but she would not lie to herself. For her sanity, she had tonight with him and that was it. And she wasn't going to spend it sobbing or feeling sorry for herself. There was time enough for that when they returned to the palace and he became immersed in duty.

He rolled away from her and rose, disappearing for a few moments before he returned and pulled her up and into his embrace. She didn't know what to say, so she said nothing. He tilted her chin back and kissed her hard, possessively, before hooking his arms behind her and sweeping her up. Then he carried her over to the bed and deposited her on it before climbing in beside her and dragging the covers up and over their naked bodies.

She was wrapped around him and she never wanted to be anywhere else. She closed her eyes and pressed her mouth to his chest, tasting the salt of his sweat against her tongue.

"I hope you don't want to sleep at all tonight," he growled, rolling her beneath him until she could feel the thickness of his cock swelling again. "Because I intend to use every minute we have together."

CHAPTER TWELVE

IN SPITE OF his best intentions, reality intruded and they fell asleep tangled in each other's arms after another hot coupling that left them both breathless and spent. It was sometime around one in the morning when Kadir woke, blinking as he groped for his phone to check the time. Out of habit, he checked for any messages from Rashid. There was nothing. It was truly over.

As if being here at the oasis hadn't already taught him that. He was about to become king, and there was nothing he could do to change it.

Emily lay curled against him, one arm thrown across his waist and a leg propped over his thighs. A current of longing slid into his bones, made his cock start to harden in spite of how many times he'd already come tonight. It would be so easy to turn her over and slide deep inside her again.

Kadir shuddered with the strength of the hunger he felt to do just that. He'd spent much of his life bedding women, but he'd never quite experienced this intensity before. He understood that it had everything to do with the situation he now found himself in. His life was in crisis, caught at a crossroads, and he felt everything strongly.

Emily had said she wanted no regrets, but he had

them. He wished he'd stripped his PA down to her delectable skin and explored her sweetness years ago. She said she would have left him, but he would have found a way to make her stay. He did not doubt his ability to have done so and he cursed himself for being so stubborn and blind when he could have had her like this much sooner than now.

He turned and glided a hand over her hip, cupped her breast. Male satisfaction filled him when her nipple began to harden. He wanted to suck it between his lips, but he didn't really want to wake her when she was sleeping so soundly.

"Kadir," she breathed, and his heart turned over in his chest. So she wasn't sleeping after all. And he was damn glad.

"Yes, *habibti?*"

"What time is it?"

"A few minutes to one."

Her breath came out as a shaky sigh. "We have more time then. I'm so glad."

He spanned her rib cage and bent to tease her nipple. "Me, too."

He was tired, but more than willing. Apparently, so was she. But instead of opening her arms to him, she pushed him until he was on his back and she straddled him.

"My turn."

Kadir lifted an eyebrow. "Your turn?"

"For once in my life, I want the mighty Kadir al-Hassan at *my* command. I want to drive you crazy, Kadir." She bent and pressed an openmouthed kiss to his chest, trailing her tongue over to his nipple and swirling around it while a sensation very like pain shot to his groin. Except it was too pleasurable to be pain. "I want you to remember me."

He fisted a hand in her hair. "I could never forget you, Emily."

How could he? She'd been with him for four long years, and while he'd been an utter fool and not taken full sexual advantage of their time together, he'd never forget the woman who had been his companion day in and day out for all that time. No, they'd not been romantic, but she'd been important to him.

The most important person to him.

He shuddered as her mouth slid down his chest. Yes, she was the most important person in his life. The one he depended on. And he was losing her. Tonight was the last night they would have alone before he had to return to the palace and take up the duties of king while he waited for the coronation.

Selfishly, he thought of keeping her with him, of keeping her in his bed and in his life—but it was impossible. She was his unsuitable bride, not at all the sort of woman the council would approve of as his queen. She'd won over many people in the palace, whether she knew it or not—but not the hardened council, who saw any woman who was not of Arab descent as highly inappropriate. They had the power to make his life—and hers—hell if he did not conform to tradition and take a Kyrian wife. He closed his eyes and cursed Rashid and his father both.

He had no right to keep Emily. She had a father who needed her and a life waiting in the States. Once she was gone, once his life settled into the routines of being king, he would become accustomed to his life without her in it. It wasn't as if they were in love. It was lust and friendship and the pain of losing someone he'd known for so long.

And that was not a reason to ask her to give up everything and remain in Kyr.

Her tongue glided around his belly button—and then her cheek rubbed against his cock and his body stiffened. She laughed softly before taking him in her mouth. Kadir had a sudden need to plunge into her mouth, to make her his this way, too, but he forced himself to remain still and let her torture him.

Her mouth was hot and wet and magical and he gave himself up to the pleasure, his eyes closing and his back arching as the sensations built inside him, propelling him to another orgasm as strong as the last.

But he couldn't bear to come this way when they had no time left. He wanted to be inside her, her body wrapped around his, her eyes glazing and breath panting as he took her over the edge with him.

He reached for her and dragged her up his body, thrusting his tongue in her mouth and kissing her hard. She knew what he wanted and she reached for the strip of condoms beside the bed, tearing one off and then breaking the kiss to roll it on before sinking down on top of him.

She took him deep, until they both groaned with it. His hands spanned her hips, gripping her hard against him, and her palms pressed into his chest as she held herself up.

"You're beautiful, Emily," he said, stunned at the picture she presented with her hair falling over her shoulders to tickle him as she leaned forward. Her breasts were high and round and her eyes glittered with some mysterious emotion as she took his mouth possessively.

She whispered as she leaned back again, "You say that to all the girls—"

But she didn't get to finish the sentence because he yanked her down and kissed her hard. And he didn't stop kissing her, or thrusting up inside her, until she shuddered around him and ripped her mouth free, gasping his name into the darkness of the tent.

He didn't let her recover before he flipped her over and rode her deeply, driving her across the bed, driving his demons before him. Vaguely, he thought he was too rough, too uncontrolled, but she gripped his buttocks and lunged hard against him when he would have slackened his pace.

It was a war, but one that exacted pleasure rather than pain. They finally climaxed together, gasping and groaning and sweating and swearing, before rolling apart and kicking the covers off the bed.

When he could speak again, he turned his head, watched her chest heaving. "I don't," he told her between breaths as anger and confusion swirled inside him.

Her gaze was puzzled. "Don't what?"

He gritted his teeth. She didn't even know. "Say that to all the girls," he ground out. "You keep trying to bring others between us, but there's no one in my head except you. No one else I want."

"I'm sorry," she said, her voice soft. And hovering on the brink of tears, he realized.

He reached for her hand, caught it in his and squeezed. He was angry with her for bringing other women into their bed and yet he'd trained her to think that way. He thought of all the times she'd escorted his dates from his suite and wanted to groan. Damn him for being so thoughtless. So arrogant.

"It's my fault. I know it. I've not behaved well."

She let out a shaky sigh. "You behaved like a rich, entitled, handsome prince. And I have no right to blame you for it. It's who you are."

A wave of anger flooded him again. And frustration. "It's not who I am," he practically shouted. "It's who you want me to be."

He shoved his way off the bed and took care of the condom before yanking on his clothes. She sat up, her eyes wide in the darkened tent.

"What are you doing?" She sounded frightened, but he forced himself to ignore his desire to haul her into his arms and hold her tight.

"I need air," he said, dragging on his boots and standing over the bed, where she sat naked and alone.

"I'm sorry, Kadir," she said, her voice containing a hint of desperation that twisted his heart. "I don't mean to hurt you."

He forced a laugh. "Hurt me? How can you possibly hurt me? I'm arrogant and entitled. And unfeeling. Don't forget unfeeling."

He turned to go but she appeared in front of him. Small, naked and fierce. Her hands fisted into his robes and hurt spiraled deep into his soul. What was wrong with him? He was like a little boy again, trying to get his father's affection and failing miserably at it.

And hurting others to do so.

"You are *not* unfeeling. And neither am I, dammit. But you scare me, Kadir. You scare me to death."

That made him pause. "I scare you? I would never hurt you, Emily. I've told you this."

"You wouldn't do it on purpose. Don't you understand that I have to remind myself of the last four years so that I can—" Here, her voice choked off and she swallowed hard. "So I can leave you, Kadir. So I can bear to go away and never see you again."

He wanted to hold on to his anger and pain and shove her away so he could stride outside and brood over his fate. But he couldn't do it. Instead, he tugged her into his arms and held her close, so close he could feel her heart beating hard and fast. She trembled and he scooped her up and returned her to the bed, dragging the covers from the floor and trying to tuck her under them.

"No, don't leave me. Not tonight. Please, not tonight."

There was a hard lump in his throat. "I won't." He disrobed and climbed under the covers with her again. She wrapped her body around him and held on tight, as if he would disappear if she let go.

He stroked her soft hair, wound his fingers in it, tried to imprint the texture of it on his skin so he would always remember. She was precious to him, and maybe it was more than just the situation that made her so. But he wasn't ever going to find out, because he would send her away tomorrow.

It had to be tomorrow. He'd intended to have her stay through the funeral, but now he couldn't bear to have her near him and not be able to touch her again. Part of him, the selfish part, told him he could have her as often as he wanted right up until the moment he sent her back to Chicago. There was nothing to stop him. They were married, and though he had to divorce her soon, they weren't divorced yet. He could take her back to the palace, spend his nights with her until it was time for the coronation.

Kadir closed his eyes and a wave of pain and loneliness washed over him. He could do that, yes. But he wouldn't. Because it would hurt her. Because she'd told him she was scared of him. He wanted to know precisely what that meant, wanted to hear her say that she cared for him, but he knew he couldn't ask her to explain. There was a veneer over this night that was so thin it hurt, but it was essential for them both if they were going to get on with their separate lives.

Separate lives. Those words were like a dagger plunged into his chest. How would he live without Emily?

He closed his eyes tight against the pain and held her close. He didn't know the answer to that question. But he knew he had to send her away tomorrow if he was going to keep from hurting her any more than he already had.

Emily woke before dawn, exhausted. But that didn't stop her from reaching for Kadir. He came into her eagerly, his body hard and ready. They did not use a condom this time and they both gasped with how perfect it felt to be joined without that barrier. He'd tried to get one, but she'd told him it didn't matter. She was on the pill.

But even if she hadn't been, she would have wanted him inside her. If she could take a piece of Kadir with her forever, she would happily do so. When she'd told him that, he'd closed his eyes on a groan and slid inside her.

His voice had been husky. "The idea of you pregnant with my child makes me happy, regardless of destiny or duty or any other damn thing anyone cares to throw at me."

They made love more gently than the night before, and when he came this time, she felt the hot spurt of his seed inside her. It made her hope, and yet she knew it was a senseless hope.

After they'd washed and dressed and had a meal of baked bread, honey, butter, fruit and coffee, they climbed into the Land Rover to make the journey back to the capital city. They did not speak much, but Kadir reached over and took her hand in his. He held it through the entire trip, until they reached the city and he needed both hands to drive again. The palace knew they were coming and sent out an escort to meet them and clear the way.

They reached the palace sometime before noon and Emily's heart clenched tight at the change in Kadir's face. He'd closed himself off, closed his emotions off, until he was once more the arrogant ruler. She thought of him last night in her arms, thought of his raw confession about his family, and ached for him.

How had she been so cruel to him? How had she accused him of not having feelings? He had them and they ran deep. Yes, she'd insisted on bringing the past into bed with them, but it had been to protect herself.

A futile hope, since she loved him so much it physically hurt. She'd thought to inoculate herself against the pain of losing him by dragging the past into the room with them, but she'd only succeeded in hurting him, too.

And now, when she wanted to reach out and touch him, she couldn't. What they'd shared last night was over. As if to emphasize that fact, he didn't even look at her as they exited the vehicle. A group of men surrounded him, bowing low, before one began to refer to a notebook he held as he spoke to Kadir in Arabic.

His new PA, she decided, her chest squeezing tight as another servant gestured to her to follow the group into the palace. When they stood inside the vaulted chamber where everyone had gathered to watch their new king return from his vigil, Kadir turned, his eyes meeting hers over the lowered heads of the assembly.

The look he gave her was unreadable, but her heart began to beat a little harder. It wasn't the look of a man who had any hope, and that made her want to scream at them all that they couldn't have him, that he was hers and no one else's.

But he wasn't hers. He had never been hers.

Emily kept her gaze on him even as he turned away and began to speak to the crowd. His voice boomed over their heads, echoed off the tiles and bounced to every corner of the giant room. She wished she knew what he said, but no one bothered to translate for her. She was already being marginalized.

When Kadir finished speaking, he did not look at her again. He simply walked away with his attendants at his side. Emily's eyes filled with tears. It felt so final, but she comforted herself that this wasn't quite the end yet. There was still his father's funeral to get through, still a few stolen moments where she would see him.

Her chest ached. Would he come to their room tonight? Or were there more rituals he had to observe? She'd intended last night to be their one and only night together, but now she knew she would sell her soul for another. She tried not to think about what that meant for the person she'd become. She was not following her own pleasure down whatever destructive path it led.

This was different. *Different.*

The pleasure she felt with Kadir was beautiful and right. She wouldn't trade a moment of last night, not even for a heart that was unbroken and whole.

She started to trail after Kadir automatically, like a satellite drawn into his orbit, but a frowning man appeared in her path before she'd taken more than a few steps.

"You must return to your quarters, Your Highness."

Emily wanted to argue with him, wanted to look down her nose and order him to take her to Kadir—what good was being a princess if you couldn't order people around when you desperately needed to?—but she didn't know if Kadir would welcome her right now. He had so much on his mind and she would not distract him from his duty.

Instead, she inclined her head and accepted an escort. But the servant did not show her to the suite of rooms she'd been sharing with Kadir before they'd gone to the oasis. He showed her to a different set of rooms, smaller, and she blinked in confusion.

When she turned around to ask the man why she'd been moved, he was gone. Her breath whooshed into her lungs in shallow pulls as she stood in the room and told herself not to panic. It was a mistake, that was all. She started throwing doors open. When she came to the closet, her clothes were not in it and she let out a shaky breath. She pivoted on her heel and started toward the door to find someone, to inform them of a mistake. The man who'd shown her to this room had clearly been wrong.

But then she ground to a halt at the sight of her suitcases nearby. She'd only traveled with one large suitcase and a carry-on, but there were two more cases sitting with the ones she recognized. She went over and picked one up. It was heavy, but she threw it on the nearest surface and ripped at the zipper.

Inside, the lovely clothes that Guido had dressed her in were packed with tissue. She ripped through the case, finding clothing, shoes and scarves. The next bag was also full, and the next. She tore them apart, sobbing like a maniac, until all the clothes were strewn across the furniture and floor.

Then she sank down on the carpet and beat her fist against the cushion of the nearest chair while she pressed her face into it and cried harder. She cried until her body ached, until her throat was raw, until she wanted to curl into a ball and go to sleep for days.

But then, the longer she sat there, as her tears leaked away, she got angry. Was this what her mother had done? Was this what sex and a dynamic lover had done to Rachel Bryant? Had she been so desperate for pleasure, for her lover's touch, that she'd given up her pride and her dignity and followed him to her doom?

Emily shuddered. She was so close to being that kind of woman right now. She would do anything Kadir asked her. Anything for one more night with him. She sucked in a deep breath, determined to get control of herself. She'd spent years making herself into a serious, professional woman. She would not lose that person simply because Kadir had turned her world so completely upside down.

She got to her feet and went into the bathroom to wash her face. Her eyes were puffy and red and she laughed brokenly at her reflection. So pitiful. But then she stared at herself until her jaw hardened. She was done being pitiful. She'd made her choice and she'd had her blissful night with her former boss.

She would not allow it to break her. She was stronger than that. She'd made the decision and she would deal with the consequences. Life would go on. She'd entered the fire with Kadir and she'd been burned. But she would not let it consume her, because she was made of sterner stuff.

Emily finished washing up, changed into a fresh dress and heels, and then she carefully repacked everything she'd strewn across the room. When it was done, when she believed that she was ready for anything, she sat down to wait for whatever came next.

When a man appeared some time later, holding a sheaf of papers, her heart sped up. But she refused to betray herself. She simply sat and waited. Whatever happened, she could handle it.

But she was not quite as prepared as she'd believed. She'd thought a heart could only break once. She discovered she was tragically mistaken. Apparently, a heart could shatter into a million pieces even after it had already done so.

"The king has signed the divorce decree, madam," the man said, bowing low. "You will be taken to the airport now."

CHAPTER THIRTEEN

KADIR NO LONGER heard what was being said to him. He'd tuned out hours ago. All he could think of was Emily. Last night with her, he'd felt things he'd never felt in his life. He kept telling himself it was the situation, the fact his life was changing so drastically, but hours after he'd signed the divorce decree, he didn't feel any better.

He couldn't stop thinking about what it had felt like to make love to Emily. He never did this. He never spent his day thinking about the woman he'd been with the night before. Sex was like eating—you ate when you were hungry but you did not think about food after you'd had breakfast. You thought about food when it was time for lunch, but not every second in between.

But it was more than sex. He couldn't stop thinking about the way she sighed in his arms, the way she felt curled up against him. He traveled back over the last four years together and realized that he couldn't stop thinking about any of it. Emily had always been there, notebook in hand, ready to organize his life and take care of what needed to be taken care of.

He'd asked a lot of her. Too much sometimes. She'd dealt with his schedule, his romances, his arrogance, and she'd never once failed him. He'd pushed her hard over the years. When she'd finally opened up and pushed back, he'd found himself wishing she'd gone head-to-head with him a long time ago.

He missed her. Dreadfully. She was his best friend and he'd sent her away.

He closed his eyes and rubbed his temples to ward off the headache threatening to crash down on him. Maybe he should have kept her and to hell with the council. She was his wife—*had been* his wife—and he needed a queen. But she hadn't signed on for a permanent job and he had no right to ask her to give up everything to stay in Kyr.

Besides, one blissful night together did not add up to a lifetime commitment. He should know that better than anyone. He wasn't a long-term kind of guy. He never had been.

If only he had more time with her, he would find out what this feeling was that had him turned upside down. He would discover the secret to why he felt so desolate over her absence. And then maybe he could conquer it.

She would be on the plane now. In the sky, flying back to Chicago. Away from him. Kadir clenched a fist as his chest grew unbearably tight.

"Enough," he said, standing abruptly. The functionary who had been speaking stuttered to a halt. And then he dropped to his knees. They all did.

Kadir looked out over the room and gritted his teeth. This was his fate. His destiny. He had no right to walk away from it. He would not walk away from it. But he would walk away right now, because he needed to be alone. That much they could give him.

"We will discuss the coronation later. Surely it can wait a few more hours. King Zaid isn't even buried yet, and I am tired."

He was already moving toward the door when the room murmured agreement. He burst out into the cool, dark hallway and started toward his room. The palace rippled around him like a giant wave, people sinking to their knees as he passed. He did not speak to anyone. When he reached his room, a guard opened the door and Kadir went inside. He didn't even get the satisfaction of slamming it because the guard tugged it closed again.

The room was strangely empty. Lonely. He went to the closet and yanked it open, knowing what he would find. Emily's clothes were gone because Emily was gone. He'd ordered it done because he'd thought it was like ripping off a bandage. Do it quick to minimize the pain.

It was, surprisingly, nothing like ripping off a bandage. It was more like digging a sharp knife into his chest and carving out his heart very, very slowly. She was gone because he'd ordered her gone. And she wasn't coming back.

It was what he deserved. What he had to live with.

He went into the private courtyard and stood gazing up at the slice of sky visible above the rooftop. This was his life now. Gazing at freedom and never having it. Giving up everything he'd ever wanted in order to do what he had to do.

If he'd been a better son, a better brother… *No.* Kadir sucked in a deep breath and told himself to stop. There was nothing he could have done differently to make his father and his brother like each other more. Or like him more.

"*Salaam,* brother."

Kadir whirled to find Rashid standing in the door to the courtyard. It was so unexpected that he did not know what to say at first. But Rashid looked tired and worn, so Kadir held his anger in check.

"I thought you were not coming."

Rashid came forward. He was still wearing western clothing: jeans and a button-down shirt. He looked a little foreign, a little out of place. A little bit lost.

"I wasn't." He shrugged and shoved his hands into his pockets. "Or not right away. I thought he was manipulating us, as usual. And I wasn't going to dance to his tune."

So stubborn, even to the end. Fury roiled inside Kadir's gut. "I tried to call you. If you'd taken the calls, you would have known it was bad."

"I shut off the phone for a few days. I needed to think."

Kadir dragged an irritated breath into his lungs. "And now you've emerged to find our father dead and me preparing for a coronation. If you had only come, Rashid. We could have worked this out."

Rashid's laugh was bitter. "Worked what out? He was always going to choose you. There was never any question. I'm not sure he ever really liked either one of us, but he found you less objectionable than I."

Kadir's jaw was tight. He was furious, but not faultless. "I'm sorry for my part in making that so."

Rashid frowned. "What are you talking about?"

"When we were kids. The horses. The dog. The hawk. All of it. Everything I ever did that you were blamed for. I confessed my crimes long ago. But I waited too late, I suppose. You were grown and gone by then."

Rashid went over and perched on the edge of one of the chairs ringing the courtyard. "Kadir." He shook his head sadly. "You thought you were the reason he disliked me so intensely? All this time, you thought that?"

"I was not a good brother."

"You were," Rashid said fiercely. "You are five years younger and you were much smaller than I was back then—did you really think our father did not know who did which things? He had spies, Kadir. Many of them. He always knew the truth."

Kadir felt as if his legs were suddenly made of concrete. He couldn't move. "Then why…?"

Rashid raked a hand through his hair. He didn't speak for a long moment. But then, when he did, Kadir was stunned.

"My mother. She was promised to another when our father took her to his bed. He married her—but then he married another soon after, and she was furious. When I was born, she swore to him that I was her lover's child." His eyes were piercing as he looked up then. "I am not, by the way. But DNA testing was not something our father would submit to then. When I was old enough, I did it myself."

Kadir could only blink. He'd never imagined… "We have different mothers, but we look alike. We look like him. Surely he could see that."

"Everyone could. But he was stubborn, and my mother was, too. They despised each other. She went to her grave claiming I was another man's son. Though not, of course, to anyone but him. I only knew because I overheard them fighting once when I was twelve."

Kadir swallowed. All this time, he'd thought he was to blame for the rift between his father and Rashid. But how could his childish antics have created a fracture so deep? He'd always wondered, but then he'd reasoned it was not up to him to figure out why. It just was. And he'd felt guilty for it.

But now Rashid was telling him it was never his fault, and he didn't quite know how to process it. "Why did you never tell me?"

"I should have."

"Yes, you should have." Anger bubbled up inside him, a well that was deep and strong and had been capped for far too long. "I've blamed myself for most of our lives. And now, when you should have been here to take your place, to make things right again, you would not come."

Rashid shook his head. "It's not my place, Kadir. It's yours. He wanted you to rule, not me."

Kadir's body was on fire with fury. He'd sacrificed so much just to get to this moment. He'd let Emily go. He'd sent her away, and now when he might have her back again, when he might have his life back, Rashid was determined to play the martyr one more time.

"Yet our father is gone, and the council has the power to decide. We will tell them what we want, and you will take the throne."

Rashid got to his feet. "No, Kadir. I came for the funeral. But you are the king of Kyr."

Bitterness flooded Kadir then, hot and sharp and metallic. "You would deny your heritage simply to win some kind of fight with a dead man? Or are you frightened to take the throne? Scared that everything he thought about you was right? That you will be a poor king after all?"

Rashid's eyes flashed. And then he growled. "If you were not my brother…"

Kadir laughed harshly. "Your brother? What does

that matter? I am your *king,* Rashid al-Hassan. And I
command you leave my presence immediately."

Rashid's face turned an interesting shade of red. His
mouth worked. But he spun on his heel without saying
a word and stalked from the courtyard.

Kadir stayed for a long time, thinking and raging inside while he paced back and forth. He was not to blame
for his father and Rashid's relationship. It was a reve-
lation, and yet on some level he had always known he
was not at fault. He just hadn't known what *else* could
be the problem, so he'd blamed himself.

He'd tried to bring them together at the end, but for
selfish reasons. He did not want to be king of Kyr. He
did not want his life to change so drastically, nor did he
want the guilt of taking Rashid's birthright.

But he was through feeling sorry for himself.
Through thinking he was stealing something that did
not belong to him. If Rashid wasn't prepared to step up
and do his duty, then Kadir would. Emily had told him
he would be a good king.

Emily. Thinking her name sent a shard of longing
deep into his soul. She made him feel like a normal
man, not a prince, not a king, not a playboy. With her,
he could be himself. He'd given her plenty of reasons
to walk out on him in the past, but she never had. She'd
stayed and done her job.

She'd finally left him, but only because he'd sent her
away. *He'd sent her away.*

Cold fear washed over Kadir as he stood in the
Kyrian heat. Emily was gone and he was truly alone.
She was the only person who *knew* him. Without her,
he would no longer be a man.

He would be a king. A ruler. A potentate.

He would have to close his feelings up and keep them

locked away. He would have no one to share a laugh with, no one to tease him about his magic mattress or his giant ego. No one to chide him for his arrogance or gaze at him with disapproval when he needed it.

No one to love him.

Kadir's chest hurt so much he had to sit down. He dropped onto the cushions and sat there with his head forward, breathing in against the pain that he thought must surely tear him in two.

It was a physical pain, yes, but it was more than that. It stemmed from the chaos in his head, his heart. His skin felt tight, his brain whirled and a wave of anguish formed into a ball in his gut, pressing hard upward. He held it back as long as he could.

And then it erupted from him in a harsh cry that rang through the courtyard and floated into the sky above.

He was a fool! Such a fool. She loved him and he'd sent her away.

Palace guards burst into the courtyard then and Kadir shot up from his seat.

"Your Majesty," one man said as they all bowed low. "We feared for your safety."

His safety? Kadir feared for his sanity if he did not act now. He snatched up his mobile phone and prayed he was not too late as he punched in the number that would connect him to his plane.

Emily was numb. She'd been numb since the moment the man in palace robes had told her that Kadir signed the divorce decree. And then she remained numb as she was ferried to the airport, as she climbed on board Kadir's private jet and waited to depart. But they didn't depart.

Instead, they deplaned and she had to spend time

in a private lounge while they waited for a sandstorm to pass before the airport could be reopened. Finally, someone came and touched her elbow and she looked up to find one of the flight attendants whom she knew from before she'd married Kadir telling her she could board now. The airport was open and they had clearance to fly.

Emily took her seat and strapped herself in. She shook her head when asked if she wanted a beverage. She slid the window shut so she wouldn't have to look at the harsh desert beauty of Kyr for another minute. So she wouldn't have to remember what it was like to spend the night in a tent with Kadir.

But closing the window didn't do a damn thing to help her forget. She closed her eyes and saw Kadir's naked body again. She thought that if she just reached out, she could touch all that smooth, beautiful skin.

Oh, she was such a fool. She'd agreed to marry him in order to help him out, in order to get the money to pay for her father's hospital bills and move him to a warmer climate. She'd thought it would be so easy. Just wear the clothes and play the part and soon it would be over.

It was not over. It would never be over in her heart. She'd fallen in love with him. Emily dragged in a shaky breath. Dammit. How could she ever forget Kadir al-Hassan? She'd spent four years with him, and though he'd made her so angry for much of that time, she'd realized that she wouldn't have been half so incensed with him if she hadn't cared about him.

The plane began to move and Emily sucked back the tears that threatened to spill free. This was it. She was leaving Kyr forever, leaving Kadir. She would go home to Chicago, sell her father's house and move him to Florida, and then she would find another job. Maybe one day she would find another man.

It hardly seemed possible when her body still ached from Kadir's possession last night. How would she ever be able to let another man touch her? Maybe crashing into a concrete embankment on a dark highway was sometimes a kindness.

Emily gritted her teeth. That was a terrible, terrible thought. Her mother died because she was selfish and uncontrollable, not because it was romantic to die with your lover rather than be parted. And hadn't Emily already decided she was not that weak?

Emily reached over and threw the window up, determined to watch Kyr slide by as the plane began to charge the runway. The palms and desert and sandstone blended together faster and faster until suddenly she could feel the ground drop out from beneath them. The plane soared into the sky and she pressed her face to the window, hoping for a glimpse of the royal palace.

But it didn't happen and she sat back again, her heart hurting with everything she felt. She would survive this, but it would take time. She picked up the remote and turned on the television across from her. She needed something to concentrate on, something to distract her. She found a movie and started it. Not a romantic movie, but a taut suspense thriller about some woman running from an organization that wanted her dead.

She'd barely begun the story when the plane banked. There was nothing unusual in that—except that it kept banking, almost as if they were going in a circle. When the nose tilted down rather than up, Emily's gaze snapped up.

A flight attendant hurried over at the look on her

face. "We are returning to the airport, madam. Everything is fine."

"Justine, please call me Emily. We've known each other too long for all this *madam* stuff."

Justine nodded. "Emily, then. The pilot says he's been ordered to return. I don't know why."

Ordered to return. Emily hugged her arms around herself as the plane descended. Soon they were on the ground and taxiing back to the terminal. Emily wanted to scream. She'd already made it through one departure. She didn't want to endure another one, though it seemed as if she would have no choice.

When the door opened, a man in palace robes entered the plane. "Your Highness," he said, bowing low. "Please come with me."

Emily couldn't move for the longest time as she tried to process this latest development. What was going on? Where were they taking her? Had something happened to Kadir?

It was that last thought that had her fumbling for her seat belt and rising on shaky legs to follow the man off the plane and into the waiting limousine. It was nearly dark now and a bloodred moon hung low over the horizon. The sky was that deep purplish-blue that happened only at dusk.

"Where are we going?" she finally asked when the car started to move.

"To the palace, Your Highness. The king commands it."

She turned her head and leaned against the glass. *Why, Kadir? Why?* Her throat ached with the giant lump forming there. How could he bring her back again after he'd dismissed her so coldly earlier? He'd sent her divorce papers and sent her to the airport. And now this.

They soon arrived at the palace. Emily smoothed her skirt and lifted her head high. And then she followed the man inside. People stopped and stared as she passed. A few whispered loudly to each other.

But then the man halted in front of a door flanked by two tall guards with swords that she was positive weren't just ceremonial. After a quick conversation, her escort turned to her. "Are you prepared, Your Highness?"

Emily blinked. He'd called her that three times now, but she was no longer Kadir's wife. It was a mistake, but one that rattled her. "Prepared for what?"

"To appear before the council."

"The council?"

He didn't answer, just flung the door wide and stood back so Emily could enter. Her legs trembled as she stood in the entry to the grand room, but she told herself it was no worse than attending meetings with Kadir in his other life. She'd often sat off to one side and listened to people fight over business while she took notes. How could this be any worse?

She went into the room and ground to a halt as she realized this wasn't a small meeting. The entire council ringed the room on a dais, their faces stern and unfriendly. Emily swallowed. But then a man stood up at the far end of the room and her eyes flew to him.

Kadir.

He looked magnificent in a black *dishdasha* trimmed in gold. Around his waist was a wide belt with a ceremonial dagger and on his head he wore a white *kaffi-yeh* held in place with a golden *igal.* Her heart throbbed with love and relief at the sight of him—and, yes, annoyance. She wanted to go to him, but she knew she could not. She remained where she was and waited for someone to tell her what the hell was going on.

Kadir stepped off the dais and came toward her and the trembling in her legs grew stronger. His face was hard and dark and beloved. He was remote and handsome and she reminded herself that she had faced this situation many times before as his PA. She'd stood beside him and not shown an iota of emotion. She could certainly do so now, even if her heart cried out for him.

"Your Majesty," she said, dropping her chin when he strode up to her. The council could not fail to approve of that, she decided.

"Emily." He reached out, and then he was tilting her chin up until she had to look at him. His eyes were softer than before and she swallowed.

"Why am I here?" Her voice was a whisper because she could not manage anything more.

He took her hand and lifted it to his lips, and her body sizzled with that simple touch. "Because I need you."

CHAPTER FOURTEEN

EMILY SWALLOWED AND warned herself sternly not to read anything into this. Kadir had said he needed her many times over their four years together. Usually he needed her to take notes, make calls, reschedule meetings. Last night he'd needed her in a different way, and while her body melted at the memory of everything they'd done together, she would not allow herself to be weak now when she'd been strong for so long.

"Surely you have people who can take notes for you."

His grin was unexpected and her heart skipped a beat. "This is why I love you, Emily. You say things to me that no one else would. You make me laugh."

Emily's lungs refused to fill for a long moment. "Please don't say those words to me. I'm in no place to take them as a joke right now."

He frowned. "I am doing this badly, then. They were not meant as a joke."

She closed her eyes and forced herself to be calm before she could look into his gray gaze again. "You're seriously telling me right now, right here, in front of a council of Kyrian leaders, that you love me?"

His frown deepened. "Bad timing, yes? I apologize, but I'm desperate."

She let her gaze drift over the gathering. They still

looked stern, but she was fairly certain they couldn't hear what she and Kadir were saying. And then his words sank in and she realized what he was doing. Still playing the game, still trying to prove to these men he wasn't a king.

"I take it your brother has arrived." She said the words dully even as her heart froze solid.

Kadir was looking at her curiously. "Yes. I have summoned him to this meeting as well. He will be here any moment."

"I see." And she did. Kadir was making one last desperate bid for his freedom. Everyone believed he was the next king, but if his brother was here, then he could formally renounce the throne in front of the council and Rashid would take it. She was here to remind them how faulty his judgment could be. Perhaps he'd even decided to insist she be his queen. That would give the old boys a heart attack for sure.

He kissed her hand again and then tucked it into his arm before leading her up to the dais and seating her in one of the chairs placed against the wall. He touched her cheek, his fingers lingering for a long moment. It took everything she had not to lean into his touch. Not to close her eyes and press her palm to her skin.

He needed her to help him once more. To get him out of a predicament. So why did he have to carry the game too far and tell her he loved her? Her soul was already broken and battered because of the last few days with this man. She didn't need to heap a false promise of love on top of the pile of rubble her life had become.

Kadir took his seat again. She tried not to look at him, but she couldn't drag her gaze from his profile. But then the door opened and another man came in. This man looked so much like Kadir that she might have sworn they were twins. Tall, handsome, yet somehow colder and far more remote than Kadir had ever been.

Rashid looked angry, haunted, and yet he also looked as if no man in this room could defeat him. No matter what anyone did to him, his eyes said, he would always win. Because, she realized, he didn't care what happened to him. She could see it in the set of his shoulders, the defiant look in his sharp gaze. He looked like someone who had lost everything and therefore couldn't care about anyone. This was the Lion of Kyr, a fierce, hard, brooding man who would as soon chew his own leg off than be trapped and tamed.

"Welcome, brother," Kadir said in English. The council swung their gazes to him, no doubt surprised that he wasn't speaking Arabic. Kadir stood and walked down the steps to the floor. Then he turned around, his arms wide, and faced the entire council. He said something in Arabic and a man hurried over to the foot of the dais.

"Omar will translate what I say, but I will be speaking in English so that my wife can understand."

Emily's jaw dropped, but Kadir kept speaking. "Yes, you are still my wife, Emily. I have rescinded the divorce decree. We are married, unless you tell me you want it otherwise."

He bowed his head a moment, and then he shook it, muttering to himself. A second later, he was bounding up the stairs and pulling her to her feet. They stood facing one another while the council, Rashid and the translator looked on.

"I will not divorce you, Emily. I love you too much. And if I am to be king of Kyr, you will be queen."

Emily's heart pounded. The words coming from his lips were so beautiful, so amazing, but she told herself not to believe them. It was a performance, and a good one. But oh, how it hurt. How much she wanted it to be real, for this amazing man to truly want her as his wife.

The interpreter finished speaking and the council started to murmur. She couldn't tell if it was an angry murmur or what because her blood hummed too loudly in her ears. She couldn't drag her gaze away from Kadir, though she desperately wanted to. She was just like all those other women, wanting him so much, wanting to believe everything he said, reading more into it than there was.

"There is another solution," Kadir continued, this time turning to face the room. He held her hand tightly in his. "My brother, Rashid, can take the throne. He is the eldest. He has no wife. His business is oil, whereas mine is building skyscrapers. A good skill, but not quite the one Kyr needs."

Rashid stood, tight-lipped and furious, but he did not speak. His arms were folded over his chest and he glared at them both. Emily knew then that this performance was as much for Rashid as for the council.

Kadir led her down the stairs and over to Rashid. His gaze flickered over her but stayed on Kadir.

"I have seen his last decrees, Rashid. He did not name his successor. He was stubborn to the last."

"He wanted us to fight over it, then." Rashid sounded bitter.

"Or maybe he decided to let us choose."

Rashid's snort said he didn't believe it for a moment. "If that gives you comfort, brother."

"It does not. But I know in my heart that you are Kyr's king. And I am your faithful servant."

Rashid's eyes blazed with fresh agony. "Kadir—"

"Take your place, Rashid. Take your nation and be the king you were meant to be."

The two men stared at each other for a long moment. And then Rashid looked over at her and Emily's belly churned.

"You truly love this woman?"

"With every atom of my being."

Emily couldn't stop the sob that choked out of her then. Both men were looking at her. Kadir seemed alarmed.

"Sorry," she said, yanking her hand from his. "I can't—I can't…"

She rushed toward the door and yanked it open and then she was running blindly down the hall in her too-tall shoes. She tripped and stumbled, catching herself against the wall. Then she reached down and ripped off the shoes, tossing them so she could run barefoot through the palace.

"Emily!"

Kadir's voice behind her sounded frantic, but she didn't stop. She couldn't. She kept running, past people who stopped and stared, past servants and delivery-men, past the dignitaries who were gathering in Kyr for the old king's funeral. Tears streaked down her cheeks, blurred her vision, but she kept running until she burst into an outdoor gallery that flanked a giant grassy courtyard ringed by palm trees. Water tinkled in a fountain at the center of the courtyard, an extravagance in the desert.

"Emily."

She spun to find Kadir behind her. The moonlight on his face revealed confusion and apprehension. Or maybe it was just a trick of the light. Maybe it was what she wanted instead of what was.

She backed away, hitting the lip of the fountain. Somehow she managed not to fall in, but what did it matter? Her dignity was already ruined. She'd burst into tears in front of him, in front of them all, and she'd failed in her performance as his wife when he'd needed it most.

"Why did you have to say that?" she demanded. "Why did you have to taunt me that way?"

Kadir came forward, holding out a hand as if trying to gentle a frightened animal. "Say what, Emily? What did I say that upset you so much?"

She couldn't breathe. She pressed her hand to her stomach and tried to concentrate on pulling air into her lungs, but it hurt so badly. "You lied, Kadir. In front of them all. You lied so your brother would take the throne."

"I did not lie." His face was a thundercloud now and she marveled at how he could be so indignant when she was the one who'd been wronged.

"You said you love me." It hurt to repeat the words, but she shook her head and continued. "You said it so the council would think you were a bad choice to rule this nation. I understand why you did it, but it's wrong to say something like that."

He came closer then, his eyes narrowed. "What if I meant it?"

She snorted. "You can't mean it."

"Why not? Because I am a player? Because I tend to pick women based on their bra size rather than their intellect?"

He somehow managed to prick her conscience. Last night he'd grown angry when she'd said something about his smooth talking. And she'd admitted to herself that he was not unfeeling. But that was before he'd used love to get what he wanted.

"I'm just your temporary wife, Kadir. And your former employee. You can't love me after one night of sex."

"No, I don't love you after one night of sex."

Her lungs deflated again. But at least he was being honest.

He grabbed her shoulders and forced her to look up at him. "I love you because I can't live without you. Because you're my best friend in the world, the one person who knows me for who I really am and who loves me in spite of myself."

"I never said I loved you." Her voice was a whisper and her pulse was a hot rush in her veins.

He smiled and there was a world of feeling in that smile. For her. "But you do. I know it, Emily. I know it because I feel exactly as you feel. As if my world would end when you walked out of it."

"That's not love. That's infatuation." She sniffed.

"I don't believe that for a minute."

Panic flooded her as old fears sprang to the fore. "But what if it's true? What if one day one of us wakes up and decides this is no longer enough? What if we want more than the other can give?"

His brows drew down, his eyes searching hers. "Why are you saying these things?"

Emily trembled. "My mother left my father when he got sick. For another man. She claimed to love Dad, but when he needed her, she left." Her throat ached. "If she hadn't left us, she wouldn't have been in the car with that man when he, when he—"

"He what, Emily?"

"He drove into an embankment. They were killed instantly."

He yanked her into his arms and hugged her tight. "I'm sorry, so sorry. But please tell me what this has to do with us."

She clutched his robes and hid her face among the folds. He smelled so good. When she was in his arms like this, she never wanted to leave. But what if she had no choice?

"What if I turn out like her in spite of my best intentions? What if I make a bad decision? What if, six months from now, you decide you've had enough of me? What will I do then? Something stupid?"

He squeezed her against him. "Other than falling in love with me, I am pretty certain you are incapable of stupid things."

"I never said I loved you."

He gently pushed her back and gazed down at her. "No, you didn't. And I want to hear it."

Panic twisted in her belly. "I'm afraid, Kadir."

"So am I. I just gave up a throne for you and maybe it was all for nothing."

She laughed, but it wasn't precisely a happy sound. "You did not give it up for me. You never wanted it in the first place."

"No, this is true. But I would have taken it to save Kyr. And I would have given it up to have you, even if having you meant ruining Kyr."

"Don't say that!" She glanced at the surrounding courtyard, worried that someone would overhear him. Surely he was committing treason to even think such a thing.

"I'm not worried. Besides, Rashid is king now. I can say what I wish."

"He agreed?"

"I didn't give him much choice, I'm afraid." He ran

his hands down her arms and bent to meet her gaze again. "We are not finished yet. I'm waiting for you to admit you love me."

Fear was a palpable thing in her chest. "What happens in six months? A year?"

"I have no idea, but I know that whatever it is, it will happen with you at my side."

He sounded so certain, so confident, but how did he know?

"If I left you now, you'd get over it."

"Eventually." He sighed and took a step back. "Emily, all I want is your happiness. If leaving me is what will make you happy, then I'll grant you the divorce. But I have no fear about the strength of our love, if you will only admit the way you feel."

"You aren't worried I'll leave you in six months? Or twenty years?"

"No." He spread his arms and flourished his palms as if showcasing the merchandise. "Six *days* with all this and you will be incapable of ever looking at another man."

Emily couldn't help but laugh, in spite of the fear still gripping her heart. "You're incorrigible, Kadir."

"I believe *delightful* is the word you are looking for."

Something gave way in her heart then, some last little lock that was holding tight to her fear and pain and binding her in chains of unhappiness. And when it did, when her heart could finally beat again, the feelings swelling inside it were all for this man. Her love was bright and hot and true and she knew it would last.

Just as his would last for her.

"Yes," she said softly, "I think that *is* the word."

Kadir dragged her into his arms and kissed her hard.

"You are mine," he growled when he finally let her breathe again. "Mine forever."

"And you are mine."

"This is a deal I'll happily accept."

They kissed under the moonlight until Kadir swept her into his arms. Emily wrapped her arms around his neck, giddy with love and excitement and sheer joy as her gorgeous sheikh strode into the palace and up to their suite of rooms.

Then he set her down, stripped her slowly and spent the rest of the night showing her just how delightful— and incorrigible—he could be.

* * * * *

A sneaky peek at next month...

MODERN™

POWER, PASSION AND IRRESISTIBLE TEMPTATION

My wish list for next month's titles...

In stores from 16th May 2014:

❑ Ravelli's Defiant Bride – Lynne Graham

❑ The Heartbreaker Prince – Kim Lawrence

❑ A Question of Honour – Kate Walker

❑ An Heir to Bind Them – Dani Collins

In stores from 6th June 2014:

❑ When Da Silva Breaks the Rules – Abby Green

❑ The Man She Can't Forget – Maggie Cox

❑ What the Greek Can't Resist – Maya Blake

❑ One Night with the Sheikh – Kristi Gold

Available at WHSmith, Tesco, Asda, Eason, Amazon and Apple

Just can't wait?

0514/01

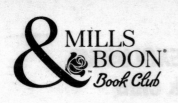

Join the Mills & Boon Book Club

Subscribe to **Modern**™ today for 3, 6 or 12 months and you could **save over £40!**

We'll also treat you to these fabulous extras:

- 🌹 FREE L'Occitane gift set worth £10

- 🌹 FREE home delivery

- 🌹 Rewards scheme, exclusive offers…and much more!

Subscribe now and save over £40 www.millsandboon.co.uk/subscribeme